D1569294

AT DARK,
I BECOME
LOATHSOME

BOOKS BY ERIC LAROCCA

NOVELS

Everything the Darkness Eats

At Dark, I Become Loathsome

NOVELLAS

You've Lost a Lot of Blood

We Can Never Leave This Place

They Were Here Before Us: A Novella in Pieces

COLLECTIONS

Things Have Gotten Worse Since
We Last Spoke and Other Misfortunes

The Trees Grew Because I Bled There: Collected Stories

This Skin Was Once Mine and Other Disturbances

AT DARK, I BECOME LOATHSOME

ERIC LAROCCA

Published in 2025 by Blackstone Publishing
Cover and book design by Kathryn Galloway English
Cover artwork by Sarah Sitkin

Printed in the United States of America

First edition: 2025
ISBN 979-8-212-17902-7
Fiction / Horror

Version 1

Blackstone Publishing
31 Mistletoe Rd.
Ashland, OR 97520

www.BlackstonePublishing.com

For Daniel Kraus

"Some nights are made for torture, or reflection, or the savoring of loneliness."

—Poppy Z. Brite, *Lost Souls*

"When we are born, we are magical and loving and full of wonder. But darkness and ignorance surround us at every corner. Until the day someone calls us a monster or a devil and we believe them."

—Philip Ridley, *In the Eyes of Mr Fury*

"There is such peace in helplessness."

—Kathe Koja, *The Cipher*

CHAPTER ONE

At dark, I become loathsome.

I wish there were a way to somehow soften the unpleasantness of it—to disguise some of the foulness, to hide some of the repulsiveness—but the horrible, wretched fact of the matter is that I become remarkably different when it's dark out.

I don't believe that I become another person, that I change entirely under twilight's enchantment, but there is undeniably a shift in my temperament, in my demeanor, in my ability to think rationally and engage with others as I usually do in daytime.

I'm not prone to committing outrageously violent, unspeakable acts when the sun goes down, nor do I deliberately hurt anyone. It's just that I become different at night. I think a lot of people are like that and don't care to admit it. I believe most people change considerably when their environment shifts. Darkness is a substantial change to our environment when you consider the implications that nighttime brings. Some things can only happen at night for this reason. People's inhibitions are lowered—their wants, their needs, their desires become paramount. That's why I only make arrangements with my clients at night. Of course, that means they never know the true me, but that's the way I prefer it.

It isn't that I loathe my clients or wish them unwell; it's simply that I don't want to give too much of myself to them. That happened when I was more inexperienced in the process—when I was far more eager to serve some people's capricious whims—and when I didn't guard myself the way I should have. I think people should remain protected when nighttime approaches, almost as if twilight were a cancer that could rot us away until we were threadbare, tattered, and broken things, never to be repaired again.

At dark, I become loathsome.

I'm sure that some of my clients expect me to behave a certain way given the outlandishness of my appearance—the large metal piercings embellishing my nostrils and bee-stung lips, my forehead with its silver horn implants, my jewelry-decorated ears, bent and reshaped to resemble the ears of an elf.

At night, I become guilty of crimes I haven't committed, much less even contemplated. I become a caricature of my former self—a creature to be persecuted, loathed, reviled, detested. At nighttime, I'm something to be tortured until condemned—someone completely and forever misunderstood.

I can't pretend I didn't summon some of these accusations, these charges, by the changes I've made to my appearance. But though humanity doesn't escape us when it's dark out, I've learned that human decency only exists when it's convenient. The rest of the time, we're feral creatures tirelessly spinning against the whitewater current of rapids bearing us down and carrying us toward an infinite black sea.

At dark, I become loathsome.

I think she can perhaps tell. Naturally, I've done everything I can to make certain she's as comfortable as possible, given the arduous demands of the ritual. This is what she wanted, after all. But she still looks at me with a bewildered expression when I motion to the simple cedar coffin I've arranged in a shallow hole in the open field where we agreed to meet.

"Are you ready?" I ask.

She doesn't answer, seeming much too preoccupied with her next destination—inside the coffin.

With the tenderness and care I deliver to all my clients, I lower her gently into the coffin until she's lying on the cushions I've arranged there and is facing me. I set the oxygen tank beside her and instruct her how to use it before I strap the mask to her face. She looks at me, and for the first time in the few hours I've known her, she appears troubled, frightened, like a convicted adulteress being led to the public square where she'll be stoned to death. Before I allow myself to think too critically about what I'm doing, I close the lid of the coffin and begin to shovel dirt on top. I wonder if she'll scream. Sometimes they do. Sometimes they beg me or plead with me to stop. But they've signed the contract and I must finish the ritual or else they won't achieve what they desire.

I don't hear any sounds coming from inside the coffin as I ladle more dirt on top of the wooden lid. Finally, when the coffin has been fully covered, I toss the shovel aside and make my way toward my van, parked near the barbed wire–wrapped fence on the opposite side of the field. I grab my cell phone from the front passenger seat and thumb through my apps until I land on the timer. I set it for thirty minutes and watch as the clock begins to slowly count down. Shoving my phone into my pocket, I lean over the vehicle's center console and open the glove compartment, where I keep a pack of cigarettes.

Tapping one out, I light the end and inhale sharply as I circle the front of the van and lean against the hood. The headlights shimmer across the grassy knoll ahead of me and reach the small skirt of tall grass that guards the distant row of trees where the forest begins. I squint, wondering if there's someone, something, with inquisitive, bead-like eyes, hiding between the trees and staring back at me, straining to measure me just as much as I'm struggling to understand them.

At dark, I become loathsome.

I can't help but wonder if whatever might be watching me from the distant trees can somehow tell—if they are keenly enough aware to know that I'm a different person at night. I'm something monstrous, something unspeakable, something appalling, something to hide away like a shameful secret. That's what I am—a secret to be kept, away from everyone, in a dark room.

I wonder if the young lady I've buried—the one who had sought me out for my expertise, my skill at performing this ritual—if *she* thinks I'm something atrocious. The way she regarded me when I prepared the oxygen tank for her . . . her face filled with such loathing, such disdain for me and what I was about to do to her. I think of proving to her just how monstrous I can truly be. I imagine myself gathering the equipment I've brought, loading it into the back seat of my van, and driving off. I think of her growing confusion, her uncontrollable panic when she realizes I'm not coming back for her. I imagine her horror—her shock, her dismay—as the air thins inside the coffin and she realizes that she's issuing her final breaths.

My own thoughts disgust me, repulse me to the point where I wonder if I'll become too sick to carry on. Of course, people expect me to be a monster, but do I need to satisfy those expectations? Just looking at me, some might assume I would be the type to bury someone alive, to trick them into willingly climbing inside a coffin only to murder them. It pains me to think there are people who expect that kind of behavior from me because of what I look like.

I finish my cigarette, crushing the burnt end beneath my shoe and squishing it into the grass. I glance at the timer on my cell phone screen. After taking a swig of whiskey from the small canteen I left on the passenger seat, I meander back toward the grave. It's at the center of the open field, the mound of fresh dirt piled like a makeshift pyramid. When the timer goes off, I snatch the shovel from the ground and start digging. The earth begins to swallow me as I scoop more and more dirt from the grave, piling the soil and debris to one side of the hole. Finally, my shovel hits something solid—the coffin lid.

On hands and knees, I clear the dirt from the coffin until it's completely uncovered. With a trembling hand, I open the coffin and come face-to-face with the young woman I buried. Her eyes are wide; she stares at me with such shock, such amazement, as if I were a welcome trespasser on some private, ancient ritual. I peel the oxygen mask from her face and she inhales deeply, eyelids fluttering.

"Can you move?" I ask her.

She doesn't respond. She seems enamored with the mere sight of me, her mouth curling into a smile. Given my appearance, it's a look I don't receive too often—a look of joy, euphoria, almost unimaginable longing. She releases soft whimpering noises as I kneel above her, one knee on each side of her torso. Her whimpers soon begin to weaken to sobs. I clear some of the wetness beneath her eye with my thumb. She regards me with such thankfulness that I scarcely recognize the woman I buried.

In an act of tenderness that shocks even me, I bend and kiss her forehead.

"Happy birthday," I say.

She still hasn't said a word, doesn't seem capable of speech. She looks at me with a strange combination of bewilderment and delight that disturbs me.

Right now, this young woman doesn't regard me as a monster. Instead, she looks at me as if I'm a sibling, a gentle steward, a devoted lover—perhaps even an immortal god to be adored, worshipped, and revered.

I don't quite know how to react to her as she takes my hands and squeezes them with apparent thankfulness. I think I should perhaps tell her, but I don't:

At dark, I become loathsome.

CHAPTER TWO

After I pull her out of the coffin, I tell her that she needs to rest for a few moments before doing anything else.

"You're like an astronaut returning to planet Earth," I joke to her.

But she doesn't laugh.

Instead, she obeys without comment, sitting in the tall grass and inhaling and exhaling with obvious labor. I make a quick dash to my van and grab a bottle of water from the cupholder. When I return, my client is lying on her back, staring at the starless night sky—her eyes as wide as quarters and her lips moving with words I cannot hear.

There's something terribly endearing about her—the way she smiles, the manner in which she regards me—and I think it's such a pity I'll never really know her. This brief encounter on the outskirts of our little Connecticut town will be our final contact. Perhaps it's best that way. That's how most of my clients prefer it, and I must confess I prefer a similar level of privacy.

She found me the way most of my other clients did, on an online message forum for those who consider themselves to be on the fringes of society: the outcasts, the miscreants, the derelicts.

Can you really change my whole outlook on life? she asked me over instant messenger one evening.

That is almost always the first question asked by those who are unfamiliar with the procedure. Granted, most people are unfamiliar with the ritual I created.

Now, I ask her, "How do you feel?"

At first, the woman doesn't seem to quite know how to answer, as though she possesses the words but cannot properly arrange them to describe her experience.

"Like . . . a dragonfly crushed between two windshield wipers," she says at last, her voice trembling a little.

I laugh.

At least she has a sense of humor about the whole ordeal, I think to myself.

Very often, those who go underground for the thirty minutes come back with a distinct surliness or a decidedly maudlin demeanor, as if I had threatened them in some way.

"That's all?" I ask.

"And . . . like a wildflower growing on the moon. Does it always feel like that?"

I shrug. "It's different for everybody."

She doesn't seem content with my half answer as she rolls her eyes. Without warning, she straightens and tries to get up. Almost instantly, her knees begin to buckle and a visible jolt of pain sends her flying back down like a balloon tethered to a wooden post.

"You'll be weak for a little while," I remind her. "Just try to be still."

"How long was it?" she asks, her eyes tirelessly searching my face, seeking an explanation.

"Thirty minutes," I say.

"Not years?"

"Was it what you had expected?"

Part of me is always curious to know how the clients react after the fact, after they've been interred, after they've been given exactly what they came for.

"I . . . don't know," she says, her eyes narrowing, genuinely perplexed by the question.

I pull my phone from my pocket and open the Notes app. I write down both of her descriptions, then ask, "Do you feel different?"

She laughs at me. "That's a stupid question." I keep typing as she continues, "I was just buried alive for thirty minutes. What do you think?"

My eyebrows furrow and my tone firms. "I have to ask. It's part of the ritual."

She blinks at me, seeming to understand.

"Yes. I feel different," she tells me quietly.

I can't help but wonder if she thinks I want to fuck her.

I don't.

It's not that she's unattractive or displeasing to look at, but she doesn't suit me, the same way that most women don't suit me. The opposite sex has never really suited me, if I'm being totally truthful. They remain a mystery to me. Men too, for that matter. I'm incapable of charming men or women.

I know this question will be the most difficult to answer, but it must be asked.

"What did you think about?"

I watch as she shuts her eyes and tightens her hands into small fists.

"Where's my purse?" she asks.

That's not an answer, and I frown, displeased, but reply, "Still in the car, with all your other things."

"Will you get it for me?"

I study her for a moment, wondering what she's planning. Humoring her, I stroll back to our vehicles, open the back door of her car, and lift her pocketbook from the floor. When I deliver it to her, she immediately starts rooting around inside the small bag.

"What did you think about?" I repeat, phone once again in hand.

"My mother . . . finding me in the bathroom," she says, pulling a small container, filled to the brim with little white pills, out of her bag.

"What did you see?"

The young woman closes her eyes, as if she had quietly been dreading the question, knowing full well I might ask it. Her lips quiver. She shakes her head, then opens her eyes; they are wet and shimmering.

"Nothing," she says, staring blankly at me. "There was nothing for me there."

I watch as she unscrews the cap of the small bottle and shakes the contents over the open grave. The pills scatter into the open coffin like the gemstones of a necklace torn from the throat of a dowager empress—a woman who had seen all the wonders of hell and knew keenly of the nothingness, the oblivion, that waited for her there.

—

The following text is an excerpt from a large manuscript prepared by Ashley Lutin and concerns the details of his "fake death" ritual. It is understood that someone reading this particular section of text will be already familiar with the ritual in question.

THE AFTERCARE

Just as there's aftercare for rough sex, there's a certain level of intimacy to be considered when conducting a ritual of this nature. Some clients prefer physical contact after they've been interred for thirty minutes. They prefer to be held while they openly cry, as if to know that another human cares for them and is monitoring their safety and well-being.

In the several months I've been organizing these "fake death" rituals, I've found that the level of aftercare for each client is highly dependent upon the client in question. Some prefer intense physical contact after they've been buried and will even petition the caregiver to engage in intercourse following their "reincarnation."[1] *It is imperative that the caregiver not engage in sexual physical contact with the client as this would diminish the integrity of the ritual as well as the honor of the overall experience.*

The aftercare of the ritual consists of three parts:

Begging

Borrowing

Stealing

I will go into careful detail of each of these subsections of the overall aftercare when tending to a person who has just been unearthed from their fake death.

"Begging" is the first stage of the aftercare program; it involves the caregiver making distinct and emotive supplications for the client to trust them and bask in their comfort. Of course, trust must be established well before this moment in the ritual; however, it's imperative for the client to know that the caregiver is someone to be trusted.

1. The term "reincarnation" is used loosely here to describe the act of being unearthed from the imitation of a final resting place created by the caregiver. The term is not meant to be taken literally.

"Borrowing" is the second part of the aftercare system. The term refers to the actions the caregiver must perform in order to properly care for their client. In this stage, the caregiver must borrow an artifact that has some sort of sentimental value to the client and utilize this prop to tend to the client's needs. If the client does not supply an article to be used as a means of proper aftercare, then the caregiver must call upon their experiences when interacting with the client and perform to the best of their abilities.

Finally, "Stealing" is the third and final stage; it refers to the fact that the client always takes a little bit of the caregiver with them when they leave. Though the caregiver can do everything in their power to make certain that their emotions and personality are guarded and protected throughout the procedure, the client will typically draw something out of the caregiver and render them changed. Just as the client transforms throughout the ordeal, so does the caregiver. The caregiver must expect to lose something to each client and must accept this loss in advance in order to properly recuperate and move on from each ritual.

The steps in completing effective aftercare are

> *fundamental to the success of the client and their caregiver. A successful aftercare denotes that both caregiver and client are forever changed by their interactions.*

—

Though I invite the young woman to sit with me in my vehicle for an hour or so, listening to music and sharing a joint, she doesn't take me up on the offer. Instead, she swiftly dodges behind her car, which is parked next to my van, and changes out of the white linen robe I brought for her. When she's dressed again in the denim jeans and flannel shirt she wore when she first arrived, she circles the vehicle and makes her way back toward me.

She passes me the robe, which I stuff back into my rucksack. I return to the hole, dragging the wooden coffin out and dumping it in the tall grass nearby. When I've done that, I start shoveling dirt into the open maw that looks to me like the mouth of an ancient deity—a deity so reviled, so loathed, by their contemporaries that they were condemned to be buried in the earth.

While I do this, I watch the young woman fish inside her pocketbook. She pulls out a small wad of cash wrapped with a rubber band, walks over, and passes it to me.

I take it and shove it in my pocket immediately.

Then she surprises me once more: She offers me her hand. Naturally, I take it and squeeze it tight in an effort to let her know that the ritual is finished, it's done—and she survived.

She leans in, pecking me on the cheek and whispering a muted "thank you" in my ear. Before I can say anything, the woman returns to her car and slides into the driver's seat. I hear the engine, see the vehicle rock slightly as she puts it into gear. I recoil a little as the car lurches forward and heads down the small dirt roadway that stretches like a dark ribbon into the nearby trees. I watch her taillights flicker through the wooded thicket until they disappear, swallowed by oblivion.

Then I grab hold of the coffin and haul the thing back to my van, where I eventually load it into the rear of the vehicle. I push aside several blank canvases that are leaning against the back seat and draped with white linen. It feels unnatural to even look at my painting supplies—relics from my former life. In my absentmindedness, I knock over a small canister of paintbrushes, scattering them across the small area. Some brushes roll out of the vehicle and drop into the tall grass. I think about leaving them there. After all, it seems unlikely I'll ever paint again. I had every intention of leaving that part of me behind.

I glance up at the night sky and notice the black velvet curtain hanging overhead like a fisherman's net. There are times when it feels as though the dark could bore holes in me the size of quail eggs—gentle reminders that I am forever changed when twilight arrives. It's strange to think that several years ago, I might have dragged the blank canvases out of the rear of the van and set up a small easel in the empty field. I might have wasted an hour or so capturing the surrounding darkness—the way in which the trees seem to bend out of respect for twilight's charm; the stillness of the sky; and how everything seems to slow to a crawl when nighttime enchants the world. I can't bear to think of taking the time to paint now. It pains me too much to consider. I once found peacefulness and tranquility in my artwork—the solitude of pushing everything away and focusing entirely on the way the tip of my paintbrush connects with the blank canvas. Now it seems like a doorway leading to a part of my life that's been locked away, closed off, forever.

I load my other equipment into the van and slam the doors shut. I crawl into the driver's seat and the motor revs sweetly when I twist the key in the ignition. I find myself leaning on the gas pedal with a sudden urgency—the same resolve that beckons all nocturnal beings to find themselves in the sanctity of the dark, to wander until daylight, to hunt under the cover of night in search of their true meaning.

CHAPTER THREE

At dark, I become loathsome.

It's a thought that comes to me quite frequently and rather naturally—an insidious little insect coiling in the darkest corners of my mind like a tiny metal spring, a well-oiled crank that spins freely and poisons the area around where it's been planted like a cancer, like a black root to spread further and further until my mind is as dark and as shiny as fresh tar.

I wonder if there's a way for me to become less despicable, less abhorrent, less nasty. But I've been this way for so long that I can scarcely recall a time when the night didn't peel from me a penance—a restitution for my vileness. Of course, I would pale, would scratch my eyes out and shuck the skin from my own body as if it were a large coat, if my wife and child ever saw what I have become. Their absence from my life is the reason I detest the nighttime so ferociously—the reason I've mutilated myself with metal, wires, and makeup to resemble the horrible creature I've always considered myself to be.

As I make the short, forty-five-minute trek back to Henley's Edge, I recall the moment that changed my life forever: when I realized that my eight-year-old son, Bailey, was missing. I had told him to wait beside the small, loaded wagon in front of the market while I went back inside to see if I had misplaced my credit card, perhaps left it on the checkout counter. I couldn't have been gone more than two or three minutes—having located the card, loose in a pocket rather than tucked into my wallet as usual—before I returned to the front of the store to find our cart unattended. Some of the paper bags had tipped, spilling from the cart and dropping fresh produce all over the sidewalk. It was dark when they took him and has been dark ever since.

At dark, I become loathsome.

I think about my purpose and how life might be if I decided to forgo the rituals. I've found a semblance of meaning and comfort in helping others who are lost wanderers—bewildered drifters spinning carelessly through twilight's dimly lit theater. Still, there's a part of me that wonders how I might feel if I turned everyone and everything away until I was completely alone with my thoughts as my only companions.

That's when I truly become loathsome—when I'm left alone. Perhaps that's what I'm destined to become. Perhaps that's how it will end for me. What's the point of carrying on this charade, pretending that I actually care more about others' problems than my own? It's served as a decent distraction, but the same emptiness always returns when the ritual is completed and the client abandons me. For one brief moment, we're together and I feel as though I've genuinely connected with another human being. I feel far more connected than I did when I was painting and showing some of my work at local galleries. But the feeling never lasts, and it always hurts terribly when they go, fleeing as if they know full well that I'm cursed, that I'm a miserable forty-three-year-old wretch marked for extinction.

What's the point of carrying on when I know it's futile? There's nothing for me here. Perhaps there once was. But not anymore.

At dark, I become loathsome.

As I drive, I think of a story I once heard about a little girl who was bitten by a snake. Her grandparents did all they could to try to save her, but she died in the back seat of their car while they were rushing to the nearest hospital.

Imagine their surprise—their shock, their amazement—when the doctors told them that she was alive.

Somehow, she had lived.

When they finally saw their little granddaughter again, she whispered to them that she had been to heaven. They asked her what she had seen—surely many magnificent wonders—but she shook her head and whispered, "Please don't make me say it."

"We won't be around much longer," her grandmother told her. "Won't you please tell us?"

"Please don't make me say it," the little girl repeated.

I think of how after weeks of their pleading going unanswered, the grandparents decided the child would tell them what she saw whether she liked it or not.

They locked her in a broom closet—hands and feet bound with duct tape and rope—and kept her there for seven days.

Every day, the grandmother would come to the door with a plate of food and ask. And every day the little girl would go without eating and say only, "Please don't make me say it."

When the child was too weak to move and near death, her grandmother pleaded, "Please. Tell me what it's like. I have to know."

That's when the little girl finally answered. "Heaven is a dark room," she said. "There's nothing for us there."

That's the only reason I haven't done anything

substantial to end things permanently for myself. Because like that child, I know that there's nothing beyond this imitation of life. There's no hope of seeing my beloved wife or son ever again. The thoughts bend into me like fishing hooks, especially at nighttime.

At dark, I become loathsome.

The following text is an excerpt from a large manuscript prepared by Ashley Lutin and concerns the details of his "fake death" ritual. It is understood that someone reading this particular section of text will be already familiar with the ritual in question.

THE PRE-CARE

There's much to be considered when first engaging with the client in this ritual of imitation death.[2] *Not only is it imperative to develop a sense of trust, a bond of community, with the client for the sake of camaraderie, but that relationship is fundamental*

2. The client must always be aware that this ritual is an imitation of death.

to the overall success of the ritual.

There's a considerable amount of "pre-care" that goes into the successful organizing and implementation of the ritual. I go into detail of each aspect of pre-care in order to ensure that those who wish to partake in or implement their own version of this activity can do so in an ethical and efficient manner.

First, the client must remove all their clothing, including undergarments, and be bathed by the caregiver in order to fully establish a sense of trust and to solidify a bond between the two, so that inhibitions are lowered completely. This is a highly necessary and fundamental aspect of the process and will determine whether the client is serious about completing the ritual.

Next, the client must dress in a white linen robe scented with lavender and jasmine. This must always be supplied by the caregiver and cannot be supplemented or altered by the client. The client may be allowed to dress in private.

Finally, if necessary and desired by the client, physical contact between the client and caregiver is allowed. This is to include only hand-holding and hugging. Any other form of physical contact is prohibited between client and caregiver, as it would significantly diminish the integrity of the ritual.

These efforts by the caregiver to establish trust and develop understanding with the client are necessary to effectively begin the ritual of the "fake death." In the several months I've been practicing these rituals, I've come to learn that those who are afflicted with severe depression are more guarded than others when it comes to certain aspects of pre-care. It's in the caregiver's best interest to find common ground with the client and establish trust so that the ritual can be as effective and as meaningful as possible.

When I finally arrive home, I stagger over a small pile of past-due bills carpeting the foyer floor.

Picking one up, I read the words *Final Notice* printed in bold red lettering on the front of the envelope.

I toss it aside and head into the living room, where I dump some of my bags and then crash into the chair angled at the television set.

My attention can't help but drift to a small pile of canvases arranged in the corner of the room—leaning there, facing the wall like scolded schoolchildren. It feels like time has frozen for those half-finished paintings—relics from a life I once cheerfully led and will unquestionably never know again. Sometimes I flip through the abandoned canvases—the various projects I left in midsentence. There's a half-finished painting of a young man I once fancied, seated on a bench at the local park. Another is a rough but nearly complete image of a bouquet of blue hydrangeas.

Of course, I've thought of tipping the canvases out, carrying them to the backyard, striking a match, and watching them burn. But there's a quiet part of me that realizes I can't bear to part with them. It's the same reason I can't bear to touch any of the money in my son's college fund. There have been times when I've thought of making a withdrawal. But I can never seem to bring myself to actually go through with it. It would hurt too much.

My fingers tap on my phone screen as I log on to a private instant messaging forum. I type in my username, *sad_boy*, and enter my password.

A number of unread private messages await me and I begin scrolling through them.

One in particular catches my attention. I can't pinpoint why, but there's a sudden need to read this note.

I need your help. Can we schedule a time to meet?—J.

At that moment, my phone vibrates with an incoming call. The caller's number appears only as *Unknown*.

I slide to answer, holding the phone against my ear.

"Hello—?"

A man's voice asks, "Is this sad boy?"

"Yeah," I say. "Are you calling to—?"

"I . . . need your fucking help," the voice tells me. Despite the pain I hear, or perhaps because of it, something draws me to this voice.

I swallow hard, preparing for the worst. "Are you in a safe place right now?"

The man on the other end of the line chuckles, amused, somehow sounding youthful. "I'm still alive, if that's what you're asking."

"Can you keep talking to me?"

"I need help," the man says, the firmness of his voice breaking apart.

"Where can you meet?" I ask him.

Without warning, the voice cuts out in a hiss of static. The call disconnects. I shake my phone.

"Shit."

It's then that I realize that the front of my pants has tightened. I sense myself firming there. Usually, I'm able to ignore this sensation. However, there was something charming about the sound of the young man's voice—something beguiling, something truly bewitching.

I've always detested the sound of my own voice. I'm frequently mistaken for a woman on the phone, which inevitably reminds me of the horrible things my father said to me about masculinity and "being a man." Part of me doesn't feel like a true man. Or, at the very least, doesn't fit the ways I've been told a man should behave and act in public. I feel as though I exist in some awful state of purgatory, trapped between both sexes.

I realize that I'm both aroused by the young man's voice and jealous of it—of the confident way in which he utters each word, every syllable. My father would have praised his brashness, had he heard the sound of the man's voice.

As I glance up from my phone, a dark figure catches my attention in the corner of the television screen. My beloved wife—Pema.

She's dressed in track pants and a monogrammed velour sweatshirt. She stands in the doorway to the kitchen. Her bald head—the only evidence of the illness that eventually killed her—is wrapped in a dark headband.

"I didn't hear you come in," she says.

I straighten, staring at my dead wife's reflection in the television screen.

"Why aren't you in bed?" I ask.

"And let you burn the lamb again?" she says, joking.

"I'll watch it this time," I assure her. "I promise. You should be resting."

"You'll starve."

I shake my head. "You shouldn't be up."

Pema's reflection flickers in the dark television screen.

"You know, in some parts of the world, they still practice mummification," she tells me. "Is that what you're going to have done to me? Or taxidermy, with a timer to remind you when dinner's burning."

I lower my head, genuinely hurt. "Don't say that."

"I'm teasing."

I rise from my chair, gaze never leaving my wife's reflection in the TV screen. "The doctor said you needed rest. You shouldn't be cooking."

"I know exactly what you'll do if you don't eat," Pema says. "Go back into the garage and turn the car on again with all the doors closed."

I close my eyes, hands tightening to fists at the horrible reminder of what I once tried to do—the incurable despair I nurtured until it ruptured and broke within me like a flooded dam, an unending wellspring of misery.

"I promised I'd never do that to you ever again," I tell her.

"Is that a new piercing?" Pema asks, as if knowing full well she shouldn't have said what she said and now eager to change the subject.

I gently touch the ring piercing my left eyebrow.

"You don't like it?"

"I never said that," she replies.

"You asked," I say. "You never used to."

Pema is quiet for a moment, then: "You seem tense."

"I suppose it's because I haven't had any *attention* in a while," I tell her, trying to waggle my eyebrows at her.

She laughs. "You have a working right hand."

I tear my gaze away from her to stare at my hand—the only thing that's willing to touch me now. I study the lines crisscrossing my palm—the wrinkles, the curves, the small forms carrying my spirit on an invisible conveyor belt I didn't ask to ride.

"It . . . doesn't feel right to touch myself," I tell her. "Seems like it would be an insult."

Pema rolls her eyes at me. "You could always go to the bar and find one of those young men you're always ogling."

She knows just how to hurt me. I sense myself cower a little, curling inward at her cruelty.

"I don't ogle them," I say to her. "You know that's not true."

"They like the *attention*, I'm sure," she tells me. "They'd be more than happy to greet you on their knees in the bathroom stall."

I shake my head. "You know I would never . . . That part of me is gone."

Pema doesn't look convinced. Her voice firms. "It isn't gone. That part of you is still inside you. It'll always be there. You can't change who you truly are."

My gaze flits from Pema's reflection in the television screen to the kitchen, where I'm met with an empty doorway.

Getting up, I hasten into the kitchen and find it empty.

The only sound is the sink faucet gently trickling.

I turn the tap until the water is shut off.

Is she right? I wonder. *Will there always be a part of me that yearns for what I cannot and should not have? Men have always been so alluring and attractive to me, but I know there is no opportunity for real love there. Men cannot love each other the same way that men and women can. I know this to be true. It's what I was taught the whole time I was growing up.*

As I head back toward the living room, I pass in front of the kitchen's screen door, which leads out to the backyard, where I suddenly notice the figure of a young boy—my son, Bailey.

Silhouette washed in the emerald glow of the overhead porch light, Bailey stands beyond the screen door like a specter. Outfitted in his mother's wedding gown—the same gown he'd often adored dressing in during playtime—he pulls down on the ruffled sleeve to wave to me.

"Dad," the eight-year-old says.

My mouth opens. I'm hardly able to speak.

"Bailey," I whisper.

Bailey's head lowers as if he is suddenly embarrassed.

"Please don't be mad," the little boy says.

I inch toward the screen door, worried that even the slightest movement will frighten my son away. "I could never be mad—"

Bailey exposes a small tear in the white gown's shoulder.

"The kids down the street tore Mom's dress," he says, voice thick with sorrow.

I swallow nervously, afraid to ask. "Did—did they hurt you?"

Bailey shakes his head. "They called me a name. The same word I heard you say."

He steps away, out from underneath the porch light. His tiny body is immediately inhaled by the surrounding darkness.

I fly through the screen door and find nothing more than an empty porch, a vacant backyard.

I look around, panting with desperation.

Without warning, Pema's bald silhouette appears in the kitchen, through the screen door. She presses her hand against the netting. Her voice is no longer soft or humorous but grating, as if her throat were filled with iron or silver.

"He heard what you called him," she says.

When I turn to look at my wife, she pulls herself away and shrinks into the dark kitchen until her apparition is no longer visible.

A blast of warm air murmurs all around—the wind carrying the secrets of long-since-dead spirits and the hope of an unearned forgiveness that may never come.

CHAPTER FOUR

From the* Henley's Edge Gazette*; published April 17, 2022

Questions Surrounding
Missing Local Boy Remain Unanswered

By Peter McNaughton, Senior Editor

Dead or alive? Runaway or abducted? These grim questions still linger in the quiet, peaceful community of Henley's Edge, Connecticut, following the disappearance of an eight-year-old boy named Bailey Lutin.

Bailey was several months shy of his ninth birthday when he disappeared on March 6, 2021. Now, more than a year following his disappearance, local authorities continue their search for the missing child.

"It's unfathomable that something like this could happen in our little town," Alice Billings, owner of the Heron Gallery, said. "I can't imagine the pain and suffering of Bailey's father. Our family continues to pray for Bailey in the hope that he will return home safely one day."

Unfortunately, the leads and tips that have trickled into the local police department over the last few months have yet to result in a credible explanation for Bailey Lutin's disappearance.

According to several sources, Bailey's father, Ashley, continues to work closely with the Henley's Edge Police Department in the effort to locate his missing son. A substantial reward is still being offered by Ashley Lutin to those with information that leads to Bailey's recovery.

Mr. Lutin, who chose not to comment for this story, remains a citizen of Henley's Edge after the disappearance of his son and the unfortunate demise of his wife, Pema Marie Lutin, who perished in early 2020 following a lengthy battle with breast cancer.

Anyone with information on Bailey Lutin's

disappearance is urged to contact the Henley's Edge Police Department.

—

It's nearly eleven in the morning when I hear the doorbell chime and I am still in bed. I smear the drool from my pillow and sit up, swinging my legs off the side of the bed and pushing my feet into a pair of fuzzy black slippers. I amble down the stairs toward the front door, where I can see a dark silhouette shifting beyond the frosted glass.

I peer through one of the narrow panes of clear glass on either side of the door and see, standing on the front porch, bathed in a bright halo of sunlight, Detective Margaret Cloade. I haven't seen her in a few months, and in my barely awake stupor, I think how much taller she is than I recall. I open the door and greet her with a half-hearted wave.

She stares at me for a moment, presumably assessing the new metal ornaments I've added to my gruesome collection since she saw me last. She doesn't show fear or disgust as some others have. Instead, she displays a decidedly morbid curiosity—an inquisitiveness apparent in each passing glance. She appears to want to fully comprehend the miserable and pathetic widower who somehow lost his eight-year-old son.

"I wasn't sure if you'd be home," she says, gesturing to the empty driveway. "I didn't see the van."

"I parked in the garage last night," I tell her. "Didn't want anybody to know I was home."

Cloade looks at me queerly. "Is now a good time?"

I stare at her, suddenly realizing she has news for me. "Have you found something?"

"Can I come in?" Without waiting for a reply, she steps over the threshold and into the entryway, which remains littered with unopened envelopes.

"Careful," I say. "Watch your step."

She follows me into the kitchen, where I motion for her to sit at the table. Cloade doesn't—just stands near the counter, shoving both of her hands into her pockets and leaning against one of the stools.

"Something to drink?" I ask. "Tea? Coffee?"

Cloade waves away the offer. "No, I can't stay too long. I just wanted to share some news."

Her words pierce right through me. I sense myself shudder a little as I study her, noticing how the corners of her lips pull downward as if preparing for a grim reveal. Before she utters another word, I know the news will be unpleasant. There's no way to soften the horridness of what must be said, so she remains somber.

"What is it?" I ask.

Cloade glances away for a moment as she clears her throat. I'm hard to look at, even for her. "We located an article of clothing buried on the edge of a field in Kent Hollow."

I swallow nervously. I can feel blood pooling and pumping in the space between my ears, hammering violently, again and again.

The detective pulls a small photograph from her breast pocket and passes it to me. I squint, holding the photo close to my eyes. As I focus, I realize it's a picture of something familiar, something I haven't seen in quite a while—a small orange hat with our town name stitched across the front panel. The hat is freckled with specks of dirt and clumps of mud, and some of the edges are tattered and torn as if the thing had been tossed into a woodchipper.

"You recognize the hat?" Cloade asks me.

Of course, I don't want to admit that I recognize the hat. Admitting that I recognize the damn thing means that what I've guessed to be true for so long is finally confirmed—my beloved Bailey isn't ever coming home.

"Bailey had a hat just like this," I tell Cloade.

Her face relaxes a little. Whether her softening is from pity or because I've confirmed her suspicions, I cannot be totally certain. Regardless, it hurts to be in the same room as the photograph. It hurts to breathe. It hurts to exist.

Cloade plucks the photograph from my hands and shoves it back into her coat pocket. With it, she caskets the remainder of my hope. Her removal of the picture almost seems as though it were a private funeral, a secret burial for a child who existed so briefly and left too quickly.

"Did you find anything else?"

From the way she stands at the kitchen counter, discomfort in every line of her body, I can tell there's something more.

"We have deputies searching the area as we speak," she tells me.

That's still not all, I can tell. There's something else. Something far more unpleasant. Something she doesn't want to tell me. I gaze at her, begging for an answer, and she seems to recognize my wordless pleading.

"We found evidence of blood," Cloade says. "Enough blood to make it seem that survival was . . . impossible."

I can scarcely believe her words. Everything around me seems to blur, the same way a transparent windscreen does when violently spattered with rainwater. I sense myself tightening while the metal piercings in my face sag obscenely, as if my skin had suddenly turned to rubber.

"You mean that—?"

"We'll keep looking," she assures me. "But our objectives might shift. We might be looking for a body instead."

She looks at me, trying to determine whether I've comprehended her. But I'm not fully present. I'm somewhere else, distant and dreaming of the last moment I saw my precious Bailey—my beloved little boy, clinging to the handle of the shopping cart when I told him I needed to run back into the store for a moment. It's strange, but I suddenly find myself struggling to remember his face—the curve of his lips, the shape of his nose, the freckles on his cheeks. Now there's a gaping black hole where his face used to be, a yawning cavity gazing back at me, threatening to swallow me until I'm a nameless thing swept toward extinction on that glittering black tide.

Cloade seems to recognize my dismay. She reaches out to gently touch my arm.

"I'm very sorry," she says. "We'll continue to do everything we can."

I know full well it won't be enough.

It will never be enough.

Certainly not enough to bring my Bailey back.

I think of the blood they found, which must have once belonged to him. I imagine it pulsing beneath me like a gentle current, carrying me off toward a godless infinity where starlight is eaten by the fanged monstrosities we build inside our minds.

—

Later that afternoon, I log on to my computer and check all my usual places—my email, the forum, the chat log. There's one place in particular I like to check every day—a private blog written by a man named Tandy.

Tandy is forty years old now, close to my age. However, he started writing the blog when he was thirty-seven. He wrote that he'd decided to create the blog when he made a very disturbing discovery about himself—that his husband's cancer diagnosis aroused him. I've been fascinated by the story from the first, and I religiously follow the posts and comment threads to see if there have been any updates.

I click on his profile and I'm delivered to his page in an instant. His profile picture is almost bland: a man with a seemingly permanent smile, pale hair, and dimples in his cheeks. He looks so average—someone you would hardly glance twice at. It seems unlikely that someone so ordinary-looking, so commonplace, could harbor such a vile and horrendous secret. At least I've had the courtesy to inform others of my disgrace through my ornate piercings. At least I've notified others that I'm an obscene, despicable thing.

I check Tandy's blog and make the unfortunate realization that there are no new comments or entries. There hasn't been anything new since last July, when someone commented that they were intrigued by Tandy's husband's diagnosis and wondered whether or not he was still alive. Tandy never replied to the comment. Secretly, there's a part of me that wishes he would. There's a part of me that yearns, that hopes he might let us know what became of his poor husband.

—

At dark, I become loathsome.

Now that I know the truth about Bailey and my suspicions are confirmed in the worst way, I find myself becoming decidedly loathsome in daylight until I'm a sunlit monster. Daylight seems to no longer be an effective remedy when it comes to my repulsiveness.

I don't go out much anymore. I keep to myself and keep my head down so as not to offend the people I pass. I still see the quizzical looks, the disgusted glances, the children pointing and tugging on their mother's sleeves.

I find myself turning my collar up whenever I walk outside—the freedom I once found in the skillful and precise mutilation of my body now a horrible, grim reminder of all I have lost. I began to add piercings to my face not long after my wife had passed, and I couldn't help but add more grotesque ornaments after Bailey was taken from me. What I once thought might bring me a modicum of comfort and release has now polluted me, making me nothing more than unusable goods.

At dark, I become loathsome.

People passing me on the street probably wonder why I have pierced my face with my various ornaments, those little souvenirs designed to test their comfort and to remind me of all I have lost.

I once watched a travel program about a small village located in South America where the villagers would pierce themselves with bits of metal or jewelry when a member of their tribe perished. I recall how the crew interviewed a child no older than seven or eight, the boy's face already snarled with glittery bits of metal. It pained me to think of how many loved ones the poor thing had lost at such a young age, but it also invigorated me to see how he kept the memory of his loved ones alive. Asked if it hurt to wear the piercings all the time, he responded, "Not as much as losing the people I love."

At dark, I become loathsome.

There's a part of me that wonders if my precious Bailey's corpse has been left to rot somewhere, withered and bloodless. I even wonder if my grieving is hopeless, given how certain Detective Cloade was during her visit. They are looking for a body. What if there is no longer one to retrieve? It's funny how horrible news you half expect can still decimate you, as if you weren't at all prepared for such dreadfulness. There is a part of me that wonders if Bailey is still alive, but to know that so much blood was recovered and that the authorities believe his chances of survival were slim has succeeded in annihilating me, destroying the shrine I've curated of Bailey in the holiness of my mind.

I wonder if that's why I've seen Bailey during some of my nocturnal hallucinations. I always expect to see Pema, given the fact that I buried her. But for Bailey there was no burial, no sign that he had perished. To me, seeing him means that he might still be alive somewhere, that his poor little spirit is attempting to reach out to me. Now I wonder if I saw him regularly because what I fear most is true—he is dead.

It can't be. I can't bring myself to believe that Bailey is actually dead. A child so young, so full of life, so rich with energy—it seems like the most egregious tragedy for such a spirited young boy to be taken and murdered so viciously.

My mind begins to invent ghastly scenarios. I think to myself, if there was blood at the scene where they recovered the hat, what does that mean? Did my sweet boy's abductor stab him repeatedly? Did my son suffer? Or perhaps the killer sliced his throat open and left him to bleed out before finally burying him in a nearby ditch.

I think of Bailey's confusion, his bewilderment—the fear he must have felt. I wonder if he pleaded—if, in his panicked desperation, he begged his captor to let him go, to return him to his father. But would he have? Would Bailey even have wanted to be returned to me?

The horrible thought coils inside my mind like a black snake and rears its nasty head at me, hissing. Although I hate to admit it, Bailey knew just how loathsome I could become. Even at the tender age of eight, the poor boy knew that his father was an imperfect and decidedly flawed man. If Bailey were given the choice, would he have chosen me as a parent?

After all, I hurt him too. I hurt him even more than his captor ever could have. I was supposed to only love him.

At dark, I become loathsome.

<masterjinx76> Hey. Are you on?

<sad_boy> I'm here.

<sad_boy> You tried calling the other night?

<masterjinx76> Yeah. That was me . . .

<sad_boy> I was going to email you. Didn't know if you wanted me to reach out or not.

<masterjinx76> I need your help.

<sad_boy> I'm here.

<masterjinx76> I haven't been feeling myself lately.

<sad_boy> Yes?

<masterjinx76> I heard you perform exorcisms.

<sad_boy> Is that what you heard?

<masterjinx76> I heard that you could change the human body until more is on the outside than the inside.

<sad_boy> I suppose that's one way of putting it.

<masterjinx76> Can you do the same for me?

<sad_boy> You're prepared for what's to come?

<masterjinx76> I need something to change me. I'm a monster.

<sad_boy> I'm a monster too.

<masterjinx76> When can we meet?

<sad_boy> I have a commitment for later tonight. But I can arrange something for next week?

<masterjinx76> Nothing sooner?

<sad_boy> It takes time to recover from each ritual I perform. You want me at my best, don't you?

<masterjinx76> Of course I do.

<sad_boy> Can you wait until next week?

<masterjinx76> Next week might be too late.

<sad_boy> Are you a danger to yourself?

<masterjinx76> I've always been a danger to myself and others. I always will be. That's why I need you. To change.

<sad_boy> The soonest I could do is three days from now. Is that good enough?

<masterjinx76> That'll have to do . . .

<sad_boy> You've read the pinned post on my profile? You know what to expect?

<masterjinx76> Yes. I've read it.

<sad_boy> You know to bring cash to our meeting?

<masterjinx76> Yes. I know.

<masterjinx76> Where are we meeting?

<sad_boy> There's an old schoolhouse on Skiff Mountain near Edgeware Drive. You know it?

<masterjinx76> Yeah. I've driven past it.

<sad_boy> There's a small field beside the schoolhouse where you can park your car. We'll meet there.

<sad_boy> I'll bring some paperwork for you to sign.

<masterjinx76> What time?

<sad_boy> Ten PM.

<masterjinx76> Ten is perfect.

<sad_boy> I'll see you then.

<masterjinx76> Aren't you going to ask for my name or number?

<sad_boy> Don't need to. I'll either see you there or I won't . . .

<masterjinx76> Do you have to go right away?

<sad_boy> Why?

<masterjinx76> I'm a little lonely . . .

<masterjinx76> Can you stay and chat?

<sad_boy> I can stay for a bit.

<masterjinx76> That means a lot to me . . .

<masterjinx76> Thank you . . .

<masterjinx76> What are you thinking about?

<sad_boy> I was thinking how if the sun exploded, we wouldn't know for eight minutes. Of course, that's not a very long time. But what if we knew? What if we somehow knew and were forced to live in agony for those eight minutes?

<masterjinx76> The sun could explode and I wouldn't care.

<sad_boy> Why's that?

<masterjinx76> My life is a concrete box.

<sad_boy> Because you've made it so?

<masterjinx76> Because that's how I chose to live.

<sad_boy> Why don't you leave?

<masterjinx76> You think it's that easy?

<sad_boy> It's because you don't want to.

<masterjinx76> There's something I do want.

<sad_boy> Yeah?

<masterjinx76> To tell you a story . . .

<sad_boy> What kind of story?

<masterjinx76> About a young man who makes a deal with another man.

<masterjinx76> If there's one thing you should know about Emil Dubois, it's that he's horrendously overweight—which would be easily forgivable, except for the fact that his clothing is too small. He resembles a child wearing a relative's hand-me-downs. He bathes in cologne and he wears pounds of gold- and silver-plated jewelry and calls himself a "gemstone aficionado." The only French he knows is the proverbial *Bonjour* and *Au revoir*, as well as a totally useless phrase, *Il a une araignée au plafond*.

<masterjinx76> "It means, 'He has a spider on the ceiling,'" Dubois says, flashing rows of yellow-stained teeth at the young man in front of him. Amused with himself, he chortles so heavily it appears as though it pains him to breathe—his every inhalation is thick and viscous sounding, as if his throat were filled with wet cement.

<masterjinx76> "Hopefully no one's ever said that to you, old boy," he laughs. "It means you have a screw loose—a spider in the brain."

<masterjinx76> What Keane Withers would give to be a spider right now—tinier than a thimble, a black velvet speck with eight minuscule pipe cleaner legs to carry him far away. Even now, despite his ignorance, he senses something isn't quite right.

<masterjinx76> Keane's gaze moves around Dubois's office—a nymphomaniac's wet dream. The walls are plastered with a peeling black-and-white mosaic of nude men and women trapped in different types of bondage equipment. Various harnesses and masks—all shiny and gleaming in the light—are pinned to the walls like trophies from exotic expeditions in faraway lands.

<masterjinx76> The air circulating in the cramped, windowless space is thick and balmy, filling Keane's sinuses with the rubbery scent of latex. Television monitors line one wall, each grainy black-and-white picture showing a glimpse into a different room of Dubois's establishment. In one image, a man kneels at the groin of another, his head bobbing up and down. In another, a man lays trapped in a swing, like a fly in a spiderweb, while a masked figure in a black rubber suit slams himself against the first man's exposed buttocks.

<masterjinx76> Dubois seems to feel as if he were a god presiding over his den of iniquity.

<masterjinx76> The room's most extravagant furnishing is a sculpture fixed into the wall behind Dubois's desk. It's life-size and resembles a human body trapped inside a black latex vacbed. The marble effigy—veiled behind what could almost match the wetness of sealskin—is obviously Dubois's pride and joy because of its location and the frequency with which he urges guests to study its perfection.

<masterjinx76> Keane's far too uncomfortable to take notice, however. Rooms without windows have always made him feel helpless, trapped. Probably because one of his first recollections from childhood involves his knuckles banging on the locked door of a steam closet at his father's hotel. He had locked himself in there by accident.

<masterjinx76> When you're nine years old, the world is your playground.

<masterjinx76> Until it's not.

<masterjinx76> He recalls pummeling his fists against the door, his eyesight blurring as the heat rose. He stripped off his clothes and pressed his face against the slit at the bottom of the door, drawing in what little oxygen he could. They found him three hours later, curled on the floor like a dying insect.

<masterjinx76> Dubois's office is as hot as the steam closet, and his company is no comfort.

<masterjinx76> "I'm sure you know I didn't ask you here to provide you with a lesson in French," Dubois says, fixing Keane with a glacial stare.

<masterjinx76> Knowing what Keane knows now, he would have never accepted Dubois's offer to chat that day. But back then he was meeker and far more polite.

<masterjinx76> Perhaps "polite" isn't the right word.

<masterjinx76> Scared to offend.

<masterjinx76> Keane used to speak with his hands covering his mouth so that people couldn't see that meth had robbed him of most of his teeth. He was always too cautious to smile, seeing the toothless grin of an infant staring back at him from the mirror. Politeness had been instilled in him to a fault as if his parents had expected his failure.

<masterjinx76> You can't blame them for thinking a college education would steer him in the right direction. The trouble was, their plan to save their only son made him want to fail them even more. After all, how many meth addicts do you know who can recite Proust down to the punctuation marks?

<masterjinx76> "I have a proposition for you," Dubois says, his lips tightening. "I believe you and I may be able to help one another."

<masterjinx76> Keane recognizes the way Dubois is looking at him. It's the same stare of enticement he uses on some of the young men at the sauna—the way the tongue gently slides across the bottom lip, the manner in which the eyes widen with unreserved intent. Dubois is obviously well practiced at this supplication. Regardless, Dubois repulses Keane, who is already rehearsing phrases he can use to turn the big man down.

<masterjinx76> Dubois is probably starved for any semblance of attention. The number of men who sleep with men in the small town of Henley's Edge is abysmal at best. Despite the fact it's been several months since Keane has had his cock sucked by a nameless stranger in one of the stalls at the public park restroom, he'd sooner starve his libido to death than fuck Dubois. Being the glutton for punishment that he is, Keane imagines the grotesquery of Dubois's expression midorgasm—the deepening of the old man's permanently frowning mouth so that Dubois resembles a decorative yard gnome, the frog-like croaks gurgling in the pit of his throat as he comes.

<masterjinx76> "You're a regular patron of the Play Pen?" Dubois asks in a way that implies he already knows the answer.

<masterjinx76> Of course, every man who is well acquainted with the prostate of another gentleman in Henley's Edge is well versed in the goings-on at the Play Pen. It is the only place in town where you can buy the latest issue of *Playgirl* after having your testicles emptied in the washroom by one of the several young (albeit unattractive) men performing services on a rotating basis for a set price. Keane himself seeks them out for companionship from time to time.

<masterjinx76> "You know very well we have an exemplary clientele with an unmatched reputation in the community," Dubois says.

<masterjinx76> Unless that reputation consists of providing patrons with an orgasm in five minutes or less, Dubois is sorely mistaken.

<masterjinx76> "There's a particular patron I'm . . . interested in," he continues. "I wonder if you've interacted with him . . ."

<masterjinx76> Keane wonders what Dubois is thinking. Sure, he's probably at the Play Pen more than some of Dubois's other clients, but Keane hardly considers himself a common whore. Dubois must sense Keane's feeling of insult because the older man stammers, his cheeks reddening.

<masterjinx76> "Please don't take offense," Dubois says. "'Interact with' can have many meanings. I didn't mean—"

<masterjinx76> "It's okay," Keane says, sparing him the awkwardness.

<masterjinx76> Dubois slides a glossy magazine across his desk toward Keane, open to a picture of a handsome man wearing an emerald blazer, with a pink chiffon scarf wrapped around his neck. His eyes are secreted behind black sunglasses with gilded frames and his cock sprouts from his unzippered fly. A small gemstone embellishes his mushroom head.

<masterjinx76> "His name's Mace Cavalier," Dubois says, pointing at the name printed at the bottom of the page. "He's been in a few amateur films. Nothing serious. Perhaps you've heard of him?"

<masterjinx76> Keane shakes his head.

<masterjinx76> The only other famous homo Keane has heard of in town is a film director who lives with his partner on the outskirts of the village. Though Keane never would have fellated "Mace Cavalier" given the pretentiousness of his name alone, it was entirely possible he existed within six degrees of cock-sucking separation from the man. Being gay in a small town is like being an endangered species in captivity, forced to procreate within a very small gene pool.

<masterjinx76> "I was sincerely hoping you *weren't* familiar with him, old boy," Dubois says. "That would spoil my plan entirely."

<masterjinx76> "Well, then, have you ever heard of the Emerald Centipede?" Dubois continues. "It's one of the rarest jewels in the world. Handcrafted from one of the finest deposits in Venezuela. It's worth millions. Once a gift to the princess of Belgium, it's been entirely repurposed, as it's fallen into—less considerate hands."

<masterjinx76> Keane feels stupid for even asking. "Whose?"

<masterjinx76> "Mr. Cavalier's," Dubois responds. "It once sat on the neck of one of the most beautiful young women in the world. Now, it's a vulgar embellishment for a certain appendage."

<masterjinx76> Dubois slides a handful of Polaroids across the desk. Each colorless photo details a different angle of Mace Cavalier's unshaven groin, the mouth of his pierced cock dripping with a jeweled centipede. The emerald head of the insect—smaller than Keane had imagined—hangs from his urethra, while the segmented body grips his shaft and extends as he becomes aroused.

<masterjinx76> "Doesn't look familiar?" Dubois asks.

<masterjinx76> Keane merely shakes his head.

<masterjinx76> "You pay for our services here, don't you?"

<masterjinx76> Of course, Dubois already knows that. He's probably watched Keane on one of his security cameras, stroking himself and creaming.

<masterjinx76> "Yeah. Sometimes," Keane says.

<masterjinx76> Keane used to think there was something sacred about letting a stranger see you naked—that there was something to be said for true intimacy. But Keane has come to realize that the bodies we possess are merely sacks of meat, pathetic suits of clay, to be used and reshaped by others.

<masterjinx76> "Perhaps we could pay you for your service," Dubois says, one of his gold fillings sparkling as the corners of his lips curl.

<masterjinx76> "What did you have in mind?" Keane asks.

<masterjinx76> "An encounter," Dubois says. "A meeting between you and Mr. Cavalier, to discuss certain things. Who's to say that conversation doesn't lead to something else?"

<masterjinx76> Dubois didn't have to connect the dots for Keane.

<masterjinx76> "You mention how beautiful his piercing is. Take time to admire it. Then, when everything's said and done, you ask him to drive you home, because you can't drive."

<masterjinx76> Keane shrinks, confused. "I can't?"

<masterjinx76> "No. You're too young," the older man says. "Do you understand? A scandal is the last thing he would want. He'll give you anything you ask for. That's when you bleed him dry, dear boy."

<masterjinx76> Keane's no fool. He wonders out loud, "Why me? You have men here who would do the job for free, just to get some action."

<masterjinx76> "Mr. Cavalier said he wants you, old boy."

<masterjinx76> "Me? But I told you—I don't know him."

<masterjinx76> Dubois wets his lips and adjusts some of the jewelry on his fingers. "I took the liberty of showing him pictures of you, and he was quite impressed. Demanded you, in fact."

<masterjinx76> Demanded? Keane cringes slightly as if the blade beneath Dubois's tongue grazed his skin, crimson welling up from the livid path his edge had opened.

<masterjinx76> "Why me?"

<masterjinx76> "Your mouth," Dubois says. "No teeth, to put it bluntly."

<masterjinx76> Keane covers his lips, embarrassed. It's clear to him that in Dubois's eyes, Keane's no better than a garbage disposal—a toothless mouth to be used. Willing or unwilling, it makes no difference.

<masterjinx76> "You'd be surprised at the audience there is for this type of material," Dubois says, gesturing to the security monitors blinking across the walls. "I make most of my money providing clients with specialized videos that satisfy their darkest desires. In fact, I have a well-paying client in Singapore who's adamant about watching young men . . . eat . . . specific things."

<masterjinx76> "You're going to film this?" Keane asks.

<masterjinx76> It's not that Keane's prudish, but he hardly considers himself a prime specimen of manhood. His chest is flat, his knees gnarled and knobby, and his cock is below average at best, even when he's feeling particularly inspired.

<masterjinx76> "You'll be compensated handsomely for your efforts, old boy," Dubois says. He brandishes a leather-bound checkbook, fumbles for his fountain pen, and starts writing.

<masterjinx76> "Tell you what," Dubois says. "I'll give you a down payment. An advance. You'll get the other half when you bring me the centipede—fully intact."

<masterjinx76> He rips out the check and passes it to Keane, who can scarcely believe the numbers scrawled across the line.

<masterjinx76> "Do we have a deal?" Dubois asks, offering his hand.

<masterjinx76> Thinking of touching the same hand Mr. Dubois uses to relieve himself—or even worse, stroke himself—nearly makes Keane retch. But politeness makes a weakling of him yet again.

<masterjinx76> Their fingers touch; the bristles of hair on

Dubois's hand tickle Keane as if he were shaking hands with a tarantula.

<masterjinx76> Dubois leads Keane to one of the private rooms at the Play Pen—a nearly empty, windowless chamber with thick, concrete walls and panels of fluorescent lighting overhead.

<masterjinx76> At least it's not a steam closet.

<masterjinx76> Keane's surprised to see Mace Cavalier is already there, waiting for them. The way he and Dubois smile at one another tells Keane they are somewhat acquainted. Keane looks around and spots the security camera fastened where two walls meet, red light flashing as it records. Dubois excuses himself before the awkward situation becomes even more unbearable.

<masterjinx76> Now that they're alone, Mr. Cavalier steps farther into the light and Keane finally sees the man in all his naked glory. The picture did not do him justice. Sometimes people don't look as attractive when they aren't wearing any clothes—they look smaller somehow, or like a caricature of themselves. That isn't the case with Mr. Cavalier, with his herculean biceps and muscular pectorals tapering to a near-perfectly defined narrow waist. From the broadness of his shoulders to the brawn of his oiled thighs, sensuality oozes from his every pore.

<masterjinx76> "Had I known you were coming so soon, I would have asked for more wine," he says, the purple mushroom crown of his cock casting a long shadow along the wall.

<masterjinx76> The jeweled centipede hisses at Keane, glinting in the light as if it knows full well what he and Dubois have planned. Keane pretends he doesn't hear it, sinking to his knees in front of Mr. Cavalier.

<masterjinx76> "Eager, aren't we?" the taller man says, patting Keane's head like Keane were a reverent dog, then cupping his chin.

<masterjinx76> Mr. Cavalier swallows hard, regarding the jeweled centipede as he pushes himself closer to Keane's mouth.

<masterjinx76> "It's beautiful," Keane says, gaze focused on the sparkling insect. "I've never seen anything like it."

<masterjinx76> "Be careful," Mr. Cavalier says. "Centipedes bite."

<masterjinx76> With that, he shoves Keane's head against his groin. Keane's open mouth swallows his engorged meat to the hilt, but it still feels like an assault. Keane chokes back quiet sobs as Cavalier stuffs his cock farther down Keane's throat.

<masterjinx76> After Mr. Cavalier finishes, emptying himself in Keane's mouth, he grabs a nearby towel set out on the floor and hands it to Keane so the younger man can clean the mess slavered across his chin and throat. Keane's surprised by his tenderness, considering the fact he just manhandled his tonsils like he were a feral beast in heat. Mr. Cavalier seems to soften, all brutishness dispelled and drooling from the tip of his deflating member.

<masterjinx76> "That was the best I've ever had," Mr. Cavalier says.

<masterjinx76> Maybe it's true. But Keane's heard that before.

<masterjinx76> His eyes dart to the camera fastened to the wall, the red light winking, coaxing him to finish the job. Before he can hesitate another moment, he makes his next move.

<masterjinx76> "It's getting late," he says.

<masterjinx76> Mr. Cavalier is already tossing on his dress shirt and wrapping his gold watch around his wrist.

<masterjinx76> "I better be on my way," Mr. Cavalier says, fingers fumbling to button his shirt. The corners of his mouth pull downward, surrendering to the cheerlessness that usually follows any orgasm—his once-eager expression now melting into a dolefulness no amount of stroking could ease.

<masterjinx76> "Maybe you could give me a ride home?" Keane says.

<masterjinx76> Mr. Cavalier's eyes suddenly avoid Keane at all costs, perhaps silently rehearsing believable excuses. He wipes the tip of his jizz-smeared cock with a rag, then tosses the rag aside with a flick of his wrist to dismiss Keane entirely.

<masterjinx76> "I would," Mr. Cavalier says, "but I'm already late."

<masterjinx76> Keane expected this reluctance.

<masterjinx76> "Dubois said you'd be happy to since I can't drive," he says.

<masterjinx76> Mr. Cavalier doesn't react at first. He's too busy searching the floor for his underwear.

<masterjinx76> "Can't or don't want to?" Mr. Cavalier asks, still avoiding Keane.

<masterjinx76> Keane pushes the words through his smile: "Last time I checked, you needed to be sixteen to get a license."

<masterjinx76> Mr. Cavalier freezes like a wild animal caught in a pair of high beams. He turns gently, as if nervous any sudden movement will upset Keane.

<masterjinx76> "You're not sixteen yet?" he asks him, eyes widening with fear.

<masterjinx76> Keane shakes his head.

<masterjinx76> Mr. Cavalier turns away for a moment, biting his lip until it turns purple. Then, "Mr. Dubois never said—"

<masterjinx76> He stops, mouth hanging open, unfinished words floating in midair. He begins to pace like an animal in captivity, his cock shrinking. Keane remains kneeling on the floor, watching the man as he paces the small room.

<masterjinx76> "Why would he have arranged this meeting if he knew—?"

<masterjinx76> Once again, unsaid words drip from the corners of Mr. Cavalier's mouth.

<masterjinx76> Keane merely watches, unsure what to say. Mr. Cavalier goes over to the small table in one corner of the room. Draped with white linen, it supports a silver platter of expensive imported cheeses and a bottle of wine. Mr. Cavalier grabs the bottle by its neck, pops it open with the nearby corkscrew, and downs a gulp.

<masterjinx76> "Fuck," he says, smearing the wine dripping from his chin. "What's to be done?"

<masterjinx76> His eyes narrow at Keane. Keane shudders slightly.

<masterjinx76> "To be done?" Keane asks.

<masterjinx76> "Something has to be *done*," Mr. Cavalier says, slamming the bottle down so forcefully that it shatters, sending glittering shards skating across the floor to Keane's feet. The wine puddles at Mr. Cavalier's feet, staining the bare concrete floor.

<masterjinx76> Mr. Cavalier looks at Keane with a wordless threat. "What do you want?"

<masterjinx76> "What do I want?" Keane asks, pretending to play dumb.

<masterjinx76> "What do you fucking want?" Mr. Cavalier asks, his fist slamming down onto the platter of cheeses. The dish jumps, cheeses rising into the air before falling back into place. "What will keep you quiet?"

<masterjinx76> Keane doesn't say anything. Instead, his gaze answers, drifting down the tall man's body, stopping at the jewelry embellishing his limp manhood. Mr. Cavalier seems to immediately understand.

<masterjinx76> "That's it?" he asks, gesturing to the centipede as if it were merely a worthless trinket at some Moroccan bazaar. "This will keep you quiet?"

<masterjinx76> Keane merely nods.

<masterjinx76> Without hesitation, Mr. Cavalier peels the emerald centipede from his cock. He cups it in his hand and admires it lovingly for a moment, his lips moving with a soundless "goodbye."

Crossing the room quickly, Mr. Cavalier passes the small, jeweled insect into Keane's hand and closes his fist around it, instructing him to forever protect the precious ornament. Mr. Cavalier grips Keane's hand tightly, his eyes trained on him with intensity.

<masterjinx76> "You'll never speak a word of this," Mr. Cavalier says.

<masterjinx76> Keane nods and Mr. Cavalier releases his hand. Keane immediately pockets the centipede, frightened he might change his mind. Though why would he? Keane and Dubois didn't exactly give him any other option. Regardless, it felt exquisite, in that instant, to be in control of another human being—to have them completely under his command.

<masterjinx76> One hand still clutching the jeweled insect, Keane watches Mr. Cavalier as he scans the area, probably looking for the rest of his clothes. He somehow looks more exposed, more fragile, without the centipede dangling from his manhood. In fact, he looks childlike—eyes wide and fearful, every movement hesitant and unsure.

<masterjinx76> Keane notices Mr. Cavalier's underwear, discarded beneath the table. When Keane kneels to grab them, his wallet slips out of his front pocket and coasts across the floor. Mr. Cavalier drops to his hands and knees, swiping frantically at the wallet. Keane flails at him, struggling to snatch the wallet from his grasp, but the taller man is far too quick for him. Mr. Cavalier flips the wallet open to reveal Keane's driver's license. He scans the card in an instant. His eyes narrow.

<masterjinx76> "Twenty-three."

<masterjinx76> The words hang in the air like a damp curtain. Both men stand up.

<masterjinx76> Keane swallows hard. It feels as though his throat were piled with gravel. "I . . . didn't—"

<masterjinx76> "You lied, you fuck," Mr. Cavalier says.

<masterjinx76> Before Keane can stammer an apology, Mr. Cavalier swings his fist and knocks Keane off his feet. Keane's head claps against the concrete wall and his eyesight blurs for a second, glimmers of light creeping at the corners of his vision. Keane's eyes begin to refocus just as Mr. Cavalier charges at him like threatened livestock and pummels him as if his body were a mere punching bag.

<masterjinx76> Keane sags to the floor. Mr. Cavalier follows, wraps his hands around Keane's throat, and begins to squeeze. Tighter and tighter. Blood pulses in Keane's head and he can hear his heartbeat between his ears. He notices the corkscrew nearby on the ground in his peripheral vision. He swats at it, fingers clawing for the corkscrew's small handle. Mr. Cavalier leans against him, his fists tightening around his throat. Keane's vision blurs in and out of focus as the other man squeezes tighter.

<masterjinx76> Somehow, Keane grabs the corkscrew and drives the tip into Mr. Cavalier's ear. The tall man shrieks, lurching away from Keane. Keane is still clutching the corkscrew, which is pulled out of Mr. Cavalier's ear, its tip dripping with blood.

Mr. Cavalier stumbles to his feet, clutching his ear and scrambling away. As Mr. Cavalier retreats, Keane coughs violently, struggling to breathe, and his vision refocuses. He pulls himself off the floor and watches Mr. Cavalier straighten and inspect his hand, looking at the blood patterning his fingers.

<masterjinx76> "I'm going to kill you, you sick fuck," Mr. Cavalier shouts, charging at Keane.

<masterjinx76> Keane drives the corkscrew into Mr. Cavalier's groin and twists his hand as if he were fastening a dead bolt. Mr. Cavalier halts, shuddering. Keane watches his head pivot, his gaze drift down to where Keane's hand is plunged between his legs. Mr. Cavalier's face tenderly softens as he slowly comes to understand. With trembling hands, he coils his fingers around Keane's throat once more and begins to squeeze. He shakes gently all the while, his lips moving with silent words.

<masterjinx76> Keane drags the corkscrew out of his assailant's crotch with a wet, squelching sound. The hole fountains blood. Mr. Cavalier's grip slackens, and before he can tighten his fingers again, Keane shoves the corkscrew farther down, impaling the taller man's testicles and ripping them apart. Mr. Cavalier releases a soft whimper, his hands dropping from Keane's throat. Keane watches as he wobbles back on both legs like a drunkard. As Mr. Cavalier staggers into the light, Keane can't help but notice his mangled crotch—his limp, half-torn cock dangling like a wilted flower to be plucked from a bed of dirt, his ball sack slashed open and sliming his thighs with dark fluid.

<masterjinx76> Mr. Cavalier sways for a moment, hands swatting at the air, before he crumples to the ground, slamming his head against the concrete floor with a vulgar thud. Keane approaches the man carefully, the corkscrew slipping from his grasp. Keane swallows hard, recognizing death as it begins to swaddle Mr. Cavalier in a permanent embrace.

<masterjinx76> Keane sprints to the entrance, fists banging against the door.

<masterjinx76> "Mr. Dubois!"

<masterjinx76> There's no response.

<masterjinx76> Keane doubles over, gagging, retching. He wipes his mouth, smearing his hand with vomit.

<masterjinx76> Just then, Dubois's voice fills the room through the speakers fixed in every corner of the small chamber.

<masterjinx76> "Well done, old boy," Dubois says. "You gave our viewers an outstanding performance."

<masterjinx76> Keane paces, the small camera fastened to the wall whirring as it follows him.

<masterjinx76> "He was going to kill me," Keane says. "You saw."

<masterjinx76> "Of course, dear boy," Dubois says. "You did exactly what you were supposed to do."

<masterjinx76> "Let me out!" Keane shouts until he's hoarse. "Get me the fuck out of here!"

<masterjinx76> The camera stirs once more, the lens shifting as it focuses on him.
<masterjinx76> "Eager to abandon your fans?" Dubois asks. "We certainly can't have our star performer leaving after exhibiting such potential."
<masterjinx76> Keane yanks on the door handle, pulling with all the strength he can gather. But it's no use. The door won't budge. Suddenly remembering, he drags the jeweled insect from his pocket and holds it up for the camera to see.
<masterjinx76> "You have to let me out," Keane says. "I have your emerald centipede."
<masterjinx76> The sound of Dubois's laugh fills the room. "Keep it, old boy," he says. "You'll be surprised to know I've already made double what that insect costs from private viewers of today's show."
<masterjinx76> "Today's show?"
<masterjinx76> "You're our next star," Dubois says. "We look forward to watching you."
<masterjinx76> The intercom clicks off, all sound vacuumed from the chamber—now Keane's precious little tomb.
<masterjinx76> Of course, there are some days when he's hungrier than others, days when Mr. Cavalier's lifeless body resembles an appetizing feast. Since there are no facilities in the room, Keane relieves himself in a designated corner, where the surf of his diarrhea spreads and pools, as black as ink.

Dubois tells Keane that views of their livestream typically go up whenever he's answering nature's call or masturbating.

<masterjinx76> Keane spends most of his days curled in a different corner of the room, admiring the emerald insect. At times he pretends it can speak and they chat for what feels like hours.

<masterjinx76> "Do it," the small creature says, coaxing him. "Look for it."

<masterjinx76> Finally, the insect convinces him.

<masterjinx76> Keane uses the corkscrew to open Mr. Cavalier's head, peeling back Mr. Cavalier's hair, greased with blood, and peering through the hole he's made. He pries the dead man's skull open as if he were an antique steamer trunk, no aspect of his victim's anatomy a secret to him any longer.

<masterjinx76> "It's impolite to play with your food," Dubois says over the intercom.

<masterjinx76> "I'm looking for something," Keane says, rooting through gray matter.

<masterjinx76> He returns to the search from time to time, when he's not feeding from the corpse or emptying his bowels. He knows what he's looking for: the spider in the brain.

<masterjinx76 has left the chat>

<sad_boy has left the chat>

As I sit there in the dark, the computer's screen washing the walls around me in a dim silver glow, I think of the disgusting story masterjinx76 has told me.

I think of Keane.

I wonder if he's still languishing in that concrete box. I think of the power Dubois holds over poor Keane. I think of Mace Cavalier—the poor man's wilted, severed cock dangling from Keane's lips as he gorges on his lifeless body.

I can't help but wonder if the young man was testing me—if he was trying to see whether I could stomach his perverseness. I think I've passed the test. After all, I never interrupted him once. I let him tell the story from start to finish. Perhaps that was his way of seeing whether or not he could actually trust me.

I sit in my chair, gazing at the computer screen, and sense my cock hardening. The feeling surprises me, especially since it's happening after I read such a monstrous and dreadful story. I can't bear to fully admit it, but something about the story excited me, aroused me. There was something about the young man's tale that turned me on.

I should ignore it, I think to myself. *I shouldn't be thinking of things like this. It's an insult to my beloved Pema.*

But I can't, or won't, prevent my hand from unzipping my pants and pulling my cock out from beneath my underwear. I sense myself becoming firmer and firmer, my dick growing as I slide my hand up and down the length of the shaft.

Why does this excite me?

I sense myself stroking faster and faster. I think of the young man and everything he told me. I think of how exciting, how alluring, it might have sounded if he told me that story over the phone—his ragged breath heating the mouthpiece, his voice trembling when he, too, reached climax. Before I realize it, I'm on the threshold of an orgasm. I let out an agonized whimper and squirt molten cream across the computer keyboard. I'm surprised at myself, shocked at my indiscretion.

I sense my body spasm as the final few ropes of fluid drain from the tip of my cock. I shudder violently, nearly retching at the absurdity of what I've done.

It all happened so quickly. I could not stop my hand from completing its mission.

It feels as if some secret doorway—some private entrance that had been closed off for eons—has been pried open deep inside me. How long has it been since I last touched myself?

I find myself breathless, panting like a dog in heat.

Something about that young man dove inside me and opened me up after so many years.

My mind returns to him over and over again. I wonder where he is right now; if he, too, pumped his cock tirelessly and thought of me. Part of me hopes he did.

However, there's another part of me that's disgusted by what I've done, by the insult I've levied against the beloved memory of my wife, Pema.

I shuffle into the bathroom, my cock dangling between my legs and still leaking like a rusted faucet that hasn't been tended to in years. I strip away the remainder of my clothing and climb into the shower stall, scrubbing myself with a bar of soap to rinse away the invisible filth of transgression. I sense myself scrubbing harder and harder and wonder if I'll peel my skin away and expose the ivory claw of bone beneath.

I loathe admitting it, but the truth is that my new client has awakened something inside me that had been dormant since Pema passed—a whisper, once closed off inside an ancient tomb, that is now screaming itself raw in the pit of my throat and eager to be heard. To me, that young man was godlike and was capable of many wondrous things.

CHAPTER FIVE

The following section of text was lifted from a private forum that Ashley Lutin regularly used to interact with his clients. This is only one of several posts that are currently available to the public.

[Pinned post]

Posted 04/13/22 at 4:35 p.m.

If you're reading this, you've likely taken to the thought that the world would be a better place without you. If you're reading this, you've entertained the notion of your demise and how much freedom it might bring you if you had the confidence to follow through.

I'm here to tell you that there's a way to avoid

these thoughts—a way to circumvent the horrible idea that your death will ease your suffering.

I've invented a practice—a particular ritual—for those who are mentally ailing and for those who have given up entirely on life. It is my sincerest hope to help those who are afflicted, who are troubled, who find themselves burdened with the notion that their existence is futile and that the world would be a far better place without them.

I've discovered that it's my responsibility to help those who are especially fragile, who are suffering from truly monstrous thoughts, and who decide that their value, to themselves or to others, is negligible.

If you are struggling with these thoughts or have suicidal ideation, I urge you to direct message me and inquire about the services I provide.

A little bit about my services:

- Length or duration entirely depends on the client and the exact services they need for a truly transformative experience.
- Cost for each client varies depending on the length of the procedure and

includes both pre-care and aftercare for the ritual.

- The meeting will take place at a private, secluded location convenient for both parties.
- Confidentiality is key and I will never share your personal information with anyone.

I ask that you seriously reflect upon the thoughts you're experiencing and consider reaching out to me to inquire about my services for those who are suffering.

Why should anyone walk in darkness alone?

—

I've never been able to envision myself beyond a certain age—as if I were marked with an invisible expiration date long before old age could claim me; as if I were undeserving of such luxury, such refinement. I always thought there was something decidedly elegant about growing old. I think of the unassuming way the elderly mill about in their bedroom slippers, the demure way in which they blow their noses, their often mild and soft-spoken manner when addressing the youth.

For some inexplicable reason, I've never been endowed with the ability to picture myself as a member of their mature and experienced coven. I can't help but wonder if my inability to envision myself as one of them has to do with the fact that I'm destined to expire before my time. I can't help but wonder if I'm somehow ordained to die in middle age and if on some subconscious level, I know that pondering my existence as an old man would be a futile exercise in total vanity.

It pains me to remember how I could never imagine growing old together with Pema even when she was alive and healthy. Even when things were well and she was in remission, I still couldn't picture the two of us as elderly—assisting one another up the stairs, pouring one another's tea. I wonder if our lives were fated to be this way—if Pema was always meant to expire at such a young, tender age because the world was undeserving of such beauty, such incomparable grace.

That was something I often thought—that the world was so cruel and unkind that the starless void claimed her, drew her back to a cosmic belt where she now lingers and patiently waits for me. Then there's my more cynical side, which knows there's nothing after our lives end and the lights go out, only infinite darkness. There's a horrible, rotted part of me that knows the truth—Pema and I will never be reunited.

I know one thing for certain: I wouldn't be organizing these rituals if Bailey and Pema were still here.

I often think about that.

I often think about what my life would be if they were still present, still offering all the love and support I need. Sometimes I hold private memorials for the life we could have lived—the happiness I could have enjoyed if they were still here. Bailey would be old enough that we would begin looking at the various private high schools in the area. Pema would probably still be working. We would occasionally take weekend vacations to Burlington, Vermont, and Portland, Maine, as we did when she was alive.

I would still be painting and shopping my pieces around to the various art galleries in the area. Was I a good painter? Of course, some probably said I wasn't. But that's beside the point. I would have been happy. Some might argue that I should start painting again if that brings me joy. But now, I'm forever incapable of feeling joy. Now, I only know darkness.

The thought of old age and my invisible expiration date circles the drain fixed in my mind as I watch the old woman's car meander up the small roadway beside the dilapidated barn. I ordered her to meet me at the abandoned Hoffman farm in Kent Hollow at ten o'clock at night and I'm delighted to find she's three minutes early. Most of my clients are everything but punctual and it's a rarity to encounter somebody who values the integrity of my time as well as their own.

She drives an old Subaru, the edges of the passenger door eaten away by rust and caked with mud. I watch in silence as the car ambles toward me and my van, parked beside the barn's silo—a massive structure pointing heavenward as if it were the pleading hand of an ancient giant forever cursed to be earthbound. Finally, she parks and her motor dims until it's quiet. She opens the door and climbs out of the vehicle and it's then that I see her for the first time, as she is lit by my vehicle's glowing headlights.

The woman is much older than I guessed from our correspondence. In fact, she's most likely the oldest client I've ever encountered. She's somewhat trim, with a short haircut that makes her face appear slimmer than it actually is. Her expression is decidedly somber; her mouth seems set in a permanent frown. Her eyes stare listlessly, seeming to confess a heritage of sadness—a birthright she inherited, a sickening trauma she assumed when she was most likely very young and naive.

I begin to make my way toward her, a little unsure how to greet her.

"You're early," I say.

She flashes me an uncomfortable smile that seems to say how much she fears what I look like—the monstrosity I've invented of myself.

"I was afraid I wouldn't find the place," the old woman says. "I wrote down the address you gave me."

I watch as her gaze drifts toward the barn and the giant, gaping hole in the side of the massive structure as if it had been bitten into, had part of the wall torn away or plowed through by some man-eating behemoth, by something other than the careless hands of time.

"We're safe here," I tell her. "We won't be disturbed."

She shakes her head. "I'm not worried about that."

"Worried about something else?"

She shoves both of her hands into her pockets and offers a small shrug. "Just a little nervous, I suppose."

I inch toward her again, forcing an imitation of kindness and testing her comfort level. "There's nothing to be nervous about. This experience is going to change your life, I promise."

She looks around, cautiously surveying her surroundings. "There's no way to stop the ritual once we start. Right?"

"There's no safe word," I tell her. "Once we begin, we have to finish."

The old woman looks a little unsettled, clearly perturbed by my exactness.

"That's why it's important you carefully consider what I'm offering here tonight," I tell her. "It will change you. But it must be endured completely."

The old woman doesn't look convinced as she crosses her arms.

"You're certain you want to go through with this?" I ask her.

Her eyes lower as she visibly indulges in a moment of quiet reflection. Then she looks directly at me for the first time.

"I'm afraid of what will happen to me if I don't," she tells me.

That's enough conviction for me, I think.

I invite her to approach the hood of my van, where I've already spread out a pile of papers for her to sign.

"Look these over, won't you?" I ask her. "Feel free to take your time to read them. I always encourage my clients to read carefully before they sign."

The old woman begins to leaf through each page, her eyes narrowing to mere slits as she scans the print.

After reading a few sections of text, she looks up from the page and appraises me.

"You're not liable for anything that happens here tonight?" she asks.

I pull out a pack of cigarettes and light one. "You don't have to sign the document. We can go our separate ways and pretend that you never reached out to me in the first place."

The woman pales, the thought of our arrangement slipping away obviously troubling her.

"It's not that I'm against it entirely; I'm just . . . hesitant," she says.

I take another drag of the cigarette, exhaling as the warmth of my breath glitters in the nighttime air. "I'm only asking for your trust for the next few hours. That's all."

The old woman regards me; there's such hopelessness in her eyes. "I just . . . want this pain to go away."

I take her hands, squeezing them. "I know we don't know each other. But I want you to know I'm going to do everything I can to change how you see the world."

She seems to think for a moment, perhaps wondering how she could possibly trust a man with so many piercings to show her how wonderful life can be.

I pass her a fountain pen. She presses the tip to the dotted line and shakily signs her name.

Then she gazes at me, knowing full well her livelihood, her safety, her whole being belongs to me.

"How do we begin?" she asks.

I fold the signed papers and stuff them into a small bag. "I'll show you."

—

The following text is an excerpt from a large manuscript prepared by Ashley Lutin and concerns the details of his "fake death" ritual. It is understood that someone reading this particular section of text will be already familiar with the ritual in question.

THE LAST WILL AND TESTAMENT

The first and most necessary aspect of divining success from this ritual involves the client handwriting an imitation of a last will and testament.[3]

3. This document may be as long or as detailed as the client feels necessary. It is not the caregiver's duty to govern what the client chooses to include in their last will and testament.

Paper and pens are to be provided by the caregiver, who also is tasked with locating a safe location where the client can consider their earthly possessions. Some clients may be disinclined to consider something so personal, so revealing; however, it is imperative to the success of this exercise that the client be as honest and candid as possible.

There have been situations when a client finds themself struggling to open and reveal an aspect of their identity during this step of the ritual. The client consequently requests the ceremony halt so that they can exit the activity before its conclusion.

Unfortunately, this is strictly prohibited, and the client has acknowledged that fact by signing the initial contract. The ritual must continue. Thus, it becomes the caregiver's responsibility to direct the client to the contract so that the ceremony can continue.

A client may become enraged when not allowed to terminate the ritual. People with depression/suicidal ideation can be quite unpredictable when it comes to their actions. As stipulated in the contract, the caregiver is allowed to utilize force to subdue the client and render them compliant for the remainder of the exercise.

The caregiver must always be on guard and prepared to take the necessary actions in order that the ceremony may be fully completed as intended.

—

After we make our way into the barn, with flashlights guiding the way, I order my client to take a seat on a small bale of hay near the building's main entrance. She obeys without comment, gaze trained on me as if expecting the very worst from me at any moment.

Moonlight drips into the open space from a massive hole in the barn's ceiling.

"You're going to write a last will and testament," I explain, passing her a pen and a blank piece of paper. "I want you to be as vulnerable and as exposed as possible."

She nods gently.

"You want an account of everything in my possession?" she asks, arranging the paper on her lap.

"The most important items," I tell her. "Things you can't live without. Items that mean a great deal to you."

The old woman's eyes lower pitifully. "Everything I once had I've now lost."

"It can be anything," I tell her. "Just be as honest as possible."

She sighs a little, gazing at the empty page, finally starting to write. I tell her that I must prepare something for the ritual and that I'll return as soon as I'm done. She merely nods as she continues to write.

I make my way back to the van and open the rear doors to reveal the small wooden coffin. I grab the coffin's handle and heave it out of the back of the van. It thuds to the ground, where I let it sit for a moment while I collect myself. Panting like an animal in heat, I grab the coffin's handle once more and drag it down a nearby path and into the small field behind the barn.

Tall grass, weeds, and various plants whip at me as I move forward until I reach the middle of the open area. I set the coffin down and open the lid, then remove the shovel I'd stored in there and begin to dig.

As I plunge the end of the shovel into the ground, sifting through dirt and soil, I can't help but think of the person who stole Bailey from me. I wonder if they dug a hole like this one, if they opened up the earth under the cover of darkness and dumped my boy's body into the pit, where worms and maggots finally claimed him. I dig faster, my shovel stabbing the ground as if I were unburying something precious, something that once belonged to me—my sweet, lost boy.

I think of terminating the ritual for the night. It would be the very first time in the few months I've been practicing that I've done such a thing. The old woman would have to understand. Naturally, she'd be upset. But what's the point in continuing? This endless charade, this useless pantomime detailing the wonders and magnificence of being a living thing. There is nothing exceptional about being alive. I know this to be certain. There's no secret meaning to our lives, no grand reason for our existence. We are merely the human equivalent of a paramecium in a petri dish. The sooner we realize that, the better. There's nothing holy or sacred about our presence on this planet. I think perhaps once I might have thought so; I might have entertained the idea that life is a peculiar and yet wonderful thing. But that was when there was a possibility that Bailey was still alive. Now there's a good chance he's dead—his blood watering the ground, his broken bones littering the land like rotted teeth.

This is when I become loathsome—when I think of the futility of our collective existence in the cosmos, when I consider how pointless everything is when I have no hope of ever seeing Bailey again. I've already reconciled with the fact that I will never see Pema again, but in my stupidity, I clung to the hope of being reunited with my son. Detective Cloade thinks there's no point. In my utter despair, I agree with her. There's no point in pretending there's any hope. Life is meaningless and it stands to reason that an eight-year-old could be, would be, lost forever. The world is nothing more than a carnivorous plant that devours the things that are the softest and most delicate.

When I finish digging the hole, I make my way back to the barn with every intention of terminating the ritual and ordering the old woman to go home. There's a part of me that wonders if she'll even be waiting for me in the barn when I return. A quiet, more cynical part of me hopes that she's already left, that she's given into her reluctance and made a quick getaway with moonlight as her only witness.

My desires are dashed immediately when I enter the barn and find the woman sitting on the bale of hay, right where I left her.

"You're still here," I say, a little surprised.

"You told me to wait for you," she replies.

"Did you finish?"

She hands me the paper. I shine my flashlight on the sheet and find there's not much written, just a few lines of chicken scratch.

In 2015, I lost the only thing that really mattered to me: my daughter. I suppose the only thing I have left to offer somebody is my heart—the very thing that continues to beat and keeps me alive. I give my heart to you.

CHAPTER SIX

At dark, I become loathsome.

The sad fact of the matter is that it's decidedly simple to infect a mind, to poison a person's thoughts and plant a seed of doubt within them that will eventually take root and flourish with extravagance. That's what Cloade did to me. Whether she realized it or not, she rooted in me the idea that my son would never return to me—effortlessly fixed it, like a wire being inserted into an electrical plug. After a year of pining, grieving, hoping—to have everything snatched away is quite possibly the cruelest sentence an authority can impose.

I've always considered myself trapped—caged within the confines of my skin, condemned to dwell in this particular body. With the discovery of Bailey's hat and blood, I sense myself shriveling further, tucking parts of myself away in the furthest and blackest corners of my mind. I'd pull my essence out of myself if I could. I'd crisp like fruit abandoned in daylight; fungus would sprout from the filthiest recesses inside me where I keep the thoughts, the feelings, the ideas that have polluted me.

At dark, I become loathsome.

I frighten myself as I regard the old woman on the small bale of hay. For the first time in months, I think of doing unspeakable things. Even worse, those thoughts, the ideas I begin to conjure—all insist that they are rooted in logic, that the poor old woman would wish me to do her harm for the sake of her agony and to efficiently put her out of her misery. How great a disservice it is for me to convince this pathetic creature that life is a wondrous and splendid thing. There's no way I believe such nonsense. How can I expect her to adopt the same thinking when we both know it's untrue?

I think of her suffering. There's suddenly evidence of her discomfort in her every gesture. The polite manner in which she folds her hands in her lap, the prim way she tucks her ashen-gray hair behind her left ear—all seem telltale signs of anguish and despair. Though she might struggle, might object to my designs, I know for a fact that she would welcome death if I offered her an irresistible invitation.

At dark, I become loathsome.

It's then that I make the horrible decision that something must be done about the old woman. In my bewitched haze, I decide that this will be the first ritual I perform where the client does not survive. Although I once believed I was helping people to discover that life is wondrous and magical, I have now realized that none of that is true.

If I truly want to help people, if I want to deliver to them a peace and an understanding that I have yet to receive, the only thing I can do is hurt them. End them.

I make the decision to put this poor woman out of her suffering. I will end her anguish by taking her life, by no longer lying to her, no longer trying to make her believe that life is a precious gift.

It's not. It never was.

At dark, I become loathsome.

—

After I seal the old woman's will inside a small envelope, I ask her to remove her clothing.

She looks at me with a bemused expression.

"My clothing—?"

"You have to be clean for the ritual," I inform her. "It's in the contract."

She looks concerned, but not enough to fight me on the matter. With a swift gesture, she removes her sweater, then kicks off her pants and shoes. Before long she's standing, completely naked, in the shaft of moonlight. I can't help but notice how her gut droops sadly, hiding some of the wiry nest of dark pubic hair covering her crotch. She raises both hands and strains to hide the large, dark brown nipples of her sagging breasts when she recognizes how I'm staring at her.

I grab a damp washcloth I've brought with me, removing it from a small plastic baggie, and kneel in front of my client. I begin to glide the cloth across her wrinkled skin. Her flesh feels like elastic, gently pulling as I move the washcloth from one end of her leg to the other.

"That feels nice," she tells me, softening at the tenderness of my touch.

I can tell it's been a while since she's experienced human physical contact since at first she seems to recoil whenever I draw close, when I push against her skin with every careful stroke. As I go on, something changes in her and she begins to let her guard down. I can tell she's starting to enjoy the experience. I can't help but wonder for how long though. Will she regret letting her guard down when I reveal my horrible plans? Will she scream, beg for mercy, ask me to spare her? The thoughts tirelessly swirl in my mind like a small fish circling in a bowl of fresh water.

Then I think of a distraction. Something to connect with her, to make her trust me even more than she already does.

"What was your daughter's name?" I ask.

The old woman's eyes lower, troubled by the reminder. "Clairice. She would have been twenty-four this year."

Although I probably shouldn't ask, I do:

"How did she pass?"

My client glances away as I scrub her neck and shoulders, gently massaging, coaxing the truth from her.

"She was driving home from class late one night," the woman says. "A drunk driver hit her and sent her car crashing into a nearby tree. The paramedics said nothing could have been done to save her. I know that's not true. There's always something that could be done."

That's the same way I feel about Bailey. I know that there's more Cloade and her team can do. It's frustrating to find them lazily passing over details as if lives were not at stake, as if families had not already been ruined.

"I'm sorry," I say to her.

"I've spent so many years wishing for the same for me," she says. "I've wanted to die and end things permanently."

I circle the cloth around her neck, imagining my hands tightening there and squeezing the life from her, leaving her withered and broken.

"Sometimes an ending is a new beginning," I say.

The old woman suddenly regards me with desperation. "This really will change my life, won't it? This ritual will make me fall in love with life again? I know there's a part of me that needs to live. I just . . . want things to change."

I recognize the shame, the hopelessness, the despair in her eyes. It's the same desolation I see whenever I stare in the mirror for too long and my reflection mutates, rippling like the surface of a lake.

"Things will change," I promise the old woman. "I'll do everything I can to make it so."

Whether she believes me or not, I cannot be certain. Despite the vagueness in her reaction, she seems to thaw quite a bit as I continue to drag the washcloth over her and clean her.

When we're finished, I swipe the white linen robe from the rear of my van and pass it to her. She goes into a dark corner of the barn and dresses herself. I wait at the building's entrance, and, gazing out into the field of tall grass stretching a mile or so ahead of me, I can't help but wonder what it will feel like to take the life of another person. I wonder if it will make me feel powerful, if it will render me as invincible as the man or woman who took my beloved Bailey.

What matters now is what's to be done with the old woman and how I can best put her out of her suffering, for the integrity of humanity. I've come to the realization that it's my duty, my honor, to wring sadness from the world, the way a mechanic squeezes motor oil from a rag, to wrench out heartache and despair in the hope of planting compassion and understanding in their place. Far too many people in this world suffer and wish they weren't alive. They yearn for the release and freedom that only death can bring—it's my honor to give them exactly what they want, to end things for them because they're too terrified to go through with it themselves.

As the old woman returns, dressed in the white linen robe I've prepared for her, I can't help but envy her. Because of me, because of my dedication to those who are suffering, she'll find herself on a voyage into another realm—an infinite chamber where it's neither night nor day, where time and reason are absent and, more importantly, unnecessary, where the constellations sing poems and sizzle hot like the dying embers of a fire extinguished long ago.

CHAPTER SEVEN

The following text is an excerpt from a large manuscript prepared by Ashley Lutin and concerns the details of his "fake death" ritual. It is understood that someone reading this particular section of text will be already familiar with the ritual in question.

THE BURIAL

This exercise is the most crucial and the most physically demanding aspect of the ritual. Prior to the client seeing the coffin for the first time, a hole, large and deep enough to completely contain the closed coffin, must be dug in an inconspicuous location where both client and caregiver may remain undisturbed. Locating this place may be challenging, and it may be some time before the caregiver feels confident enough to execute a ritual in general. Despite these difficulties, the caregiver must locate a well-camouflaged site that will foster camaraderie and communion between both parties.

After the burial site is prepared by the caregiver, the client must be led to the area where they will be interred. At this moment, the caregiver must instruct the client to lie down inside the coffin and prepare themself for burial. An oxygen mask and tank will be supplied for those who are especially nervous about the procedure and who might be prone to anxiety or panic attacks throughout the thirty minutes of entombment. This will be determined via correspondence prior to meeting for the ritual.

After the client is prepared for interment, the coffin lid must be closed, and the grave should be filled with dirt by the caregiver. In my experience, it's at this moment that clients typically express their fear or dissatisfaction, their anxiety about continuing the ritual. It's the caregiver's responsibility to ignore any pleas or supplications from the client and carry on as if they were conducting a typical burial, where the client is deceased.

When the grave is filled with dirt and the coffin is completely covered, the caregiver will set a timer for thirty minutes. During this time, the caregiver should rest and recover from the exertion of filling the grave, which is a physically demanding activity. At the end of the thirty minutes, the caregiver will unearth the coffin.

Since digging the hole, as well as burying and exhuming the coffin, is a physically taxing activity, especially when executed by a single individual during a short span of time, the caregiver's health and well-being must always take precedence. If anything should happen to the caregiver during the burial or the exhumation, the client would perish.

Midnight's breath clings to us as we slowly make our way from the barn and into the field of tall grass. Weeds and other plants crunch beneath our feet as we march single file down a narrow pathway toward the burial site I've arranged. Night's perfume—an intoxicating aroma of bewitching smells that is somehow incapable of disguising the unpleasantness of the task at hand—surrounds us.

I imagine an invisible wreath of twilight's aroma beading on the old woman's skin like glimmering pellets of morning dew—as if nighttime were marking her, the way it seems to mark all who are acolytes of the stars.

As we move down the pathway, I think of the many ways I could end my client's suffering right now, before we even reach the burial site. I don't think of it as killing her—the word *killing* has so many weighted complications and connotations attached. I've already convinced myself that her burial will not be murder. Instead, it will be a peaceful end to a troubled and pain-filled existence. I want that so badly for her. I'm certain that she yearns, as I do, for release from her agony, for freedom from her lifetime of suffering.

And why shouldn't she?

After all, what else does she have to live for?

Nothing.

There's nothing left for her in this world and every day that she carries on as if she's well, as if she's not hurting terribly, is a burden on her mental health. I'm doing this to save her, to spare her the agony I endure day in and day out. Others may not view what I'm about to do as saving her, as helping her in any way. But their opinions don't matter to me.

What matters most of all to me is coaxing her into

the coffin so that I can bury her and leave her there for death's sweet embrace to claim her. Naturally, there will be a few moments when she suffers—when she runs out of oxygen, when she claws at the coffin lid and begs to be released, when fear overtakes her and breaks her down. Regardless, I know that this pain will be short-lived. Her suffering will end soon enough, thanks to me.

Finally, we reach the burial site in the center of the open field. The coffin has already been lowered into the grave and I've arranged the small oxygen tank beside the coffin lid.

"You'll be in there for a little over thirty minutes," I remind her, "since I don't start the stopwatch until the coffin is completely buried."

The old woman looks at me, unsure. "What if something happens—?"

"Like what?" I ask her.

The old woman seems to search her mind for an excuse, anything that she can use to backpedal and worm her way out of the contract she signed.

"I've never had issues with any of my clients," I say. "All I ask is that you trust me. Can you do that?"

The woman swallows nervously. She nods, perhaps a little reluctant but obviously eager to finally place her trust in something, someone, worthy. If only she knew the plans I have in store for her.

Steadying herself by leaning against my shoulder, the woman kneels and crawls into the grave. It feels like hours before she finally settles into the open coffin. Eyes wide, she looks up at me, her lips moving without sound, perhaps silently praying and begging God to give her the strength to complete her ordeal.

If only she knew that she never had a choice.

I offer her the oxygen mask and tank.

"Do you think you'll need this?"

She waves me away.

"I think I should experience it without help," she says.

I can't help but admire her nerve. I smile at her, setting the oxygen tank aside. Just as I'm about to close the coffin, I notice that the old woman's eyes are glittering with wetness. Her mouth opens.

"Something wrong?" I ask.

She shakes her head, then begins to speak.

"When I was little, our mother brought home a dog for us to keep as a pet. My father didn't take to the idea. He didn't like the thought of keeping an animal in the house. Nothing was ever clean enough for him."

I watch as the old woman wipes some of the dampness from beneath her eyes.

"One day, he found the dog had taken a giant shit on the newly pressed suit he had left lying on the bed," she continues. "So, he took a baseball bat and hit the dog on the side of the head. The dog didn't die; it just sort of wobbled there for a moment, then collapsed. My father walked away.

"We didn't keep the dog for very long after that. A family moved in down the street, and for some reason, they offered to adopt him. They asked us why the poor thing limped and why its left eye was always bloodshot, but we didn't give them an answer."

The woman clears a catch in her throat, coughing a little.

"A few years later, I asked my father why he had done that to that poor creature," she says. "I asked him what made him do something so monstrous. He wasn't a violent man. He never hit any of his children. Never struck our mother. Why did he hurt a dog that didn't know any better?

"He looked at me queerly, as if I should know better than to ask, and said: 'If I didn't hurt that dog, he would've taken a shit on my clothes every day until he died.' He must have seen that I didn't understand, because he then told me: 'Sometimes pain is earned.'"

I tilt my head, puzzled. She seems to recognize my expression despite the metal studding my face.

"I've done this to myself," she says. "This is the grave I've built for myself and it's what I deserve. You see, when we begin our lives in this world, we begin as creators. We are constantly building. Our lives are spent creating, inventing, designing. I always knew I was building something, starting when I was very little. I only wish I had known it was a grave. My grave."

I soften, realizing exactly what she means. I wish I could offer her a semblance of hope, a modicum of pity, but actions speak louder than words. Anything I could have the gall to say wouldn't be enough for her now. All I can do is close the coffin lid and bury her like a dirty secret.

For the first time, I feel reluctance to close the coffin. I wonder if my hesitancy stems from pity or from the fact that I know full well that this coffin will never be opened again. I will be the last person to see this poor, pathetic old woman alive.

Before another moment of hesitation, I drag the lid over the coffin and close it. I snatch up the nearby shovel and begin to ladle dirt on top of the coffin. I wonder, if shoveling were soundless, if I would hear the old woman pleading, begging me to stop, demanding

I cease the ritual and return her to the world aboveground. But digging is not silent, nor do I intend to listen for her. Instead, I plug my ears with my earbuds, scroll to the Music app on my phone, and start playing the first song that pops onto my screen. Any noises, any screams, that might issue from the hole in the ground will not reach me, will not reason with me to stop what I'm doing.

Faster and faster, I scoop dirt from the pile beside me and toss it into the grave, blanketing the coffin until it's completely covered. When I'm finished, I take out my earbuds, catch my breath, and fling the shovel aside. As I stand there in the open field, the gentle whisper of midnight murmuring all around me, I sense the faintest hum of a heartbeat pulsing beneath my feet—a horrible secret, dimmed like the flame of a flickering candle.

I feel no sadness or remorse for the woman I've buried six feet beneath me. Instead, I yearn for the same resolution. I long to be cradled by the hands of darkness, to be fed into the gaping maw of infinity, where the human body is a lyric that the nighttime sings again and again until apocalypse enters with music to drown out the symphony of our suffering.

—

When I'm finished covering the burial site with weeds and flowers, I swipe the dirt-caked shovel from the ground and trek back from the center of the field to the barn. As I stroll along, I think of my client and how calm she must be at this very moment, resting in the dark, certain that I will soon return for her. There's something so calming, so peaceful, about being blanketed in total darkness. Although I recognize the fact that at dark, I become loathsome, I can't deny there's something exquisite about darkness and how it keeps our most precious secrets hidden in a celestial vault.

I wonder when my client's calmness will harden to panic, when she will realize I'm not coming back. I won't be attending her gravesite again, won't retrieve her from the earth, won't save her from the royal kingdom of worms and maggots even now coiling around her in a frenzied blur. I wonder if she'll scream, if she'll pound on the coffin lid and strain to climb out of the grave I prepared. Of course, there will be a moment when she will realize her pleading is futile. The Hoffman farm covers nearly fifty acres and has been undisturbed since the late 1990s, when the last Hoffman perished in a plane crash. There was no proper heir and different factions have been battling over the land ever since.

Once I arrive where we parked our vehicles, I open

the driver's-side door of the old woman's car and search for her keys, from the vehicle's center console to the glove compartment. Nothing. I pull down the sun visor and her keys scatter on the car seat with a vulgar thud. *Finally*, I think.

I lurch into the driver's seat, shove the keys into the ignition, and listen to the motor purr as I press my foot onto the accelerator. Shifting the car into gear, I steer the vehicle down a nearby path that leads into the dark forest. After careering along for a few hundred yards, when I'm certain the car cannot be seen from the main road, I shut off the headlights and kill the engine. When I climb out of the vehicle, the entire forest surrounding me seems to murmur, contemplating the arrival of a visitor who clearly does not belong and, even worse, is not entirely welcome.

Before I allow my mind to wander too freely, I dash out of the thicket and return to my van. I curse myself for wasting a perfectly good coffin on the old woman; after all, I have another client lined up for tomorrow night. But I wouldn't have been able to bury her without the coffin—she surely would have rebelled at the thought of being shoved bodily into an empty hole.

I wonder if I can return to the person I bought the coffin from or if he'd suspect something is amiss. I got the wooden box from a mortician who lives a few towns over from Henley's Edge. He checked in on me from time to time after Pema passed away and he'd handled her funeral. I expect he'll be glad to provide another coffin, but it's likely he'll ask what became of the first one he sold me. I can't have that.

The first soul I've saved is now behind me, buried in the field of tall grass, never to be exhumed. As I lunge into the driver's seat of my van and jam my keys into the ignition, I think of the story the old woman told me before I buried her, of how she said that "pain is earned." If that is true, then I must deserve a century's worth of agony for what I did to my sweet Bailey.

Burying the old woman alive and putting her out of her misery was my reckoning, my atonement. That much is now very clear to me. This is why I've been put on this earth; this is why I've suffered for so long. I'm here to provide an escape, to set free those who are burdened with despair, who are saddled with hopelessness. I'm here to set those poor souls free and cast them into oblivion, where pain will no longer trouble them. However, the question gnaws at me, the question I dare not answer: Who will bury me when my time comes?

CHAPTER EIGHT

At dark, I become loathsome.

I can't help but wonder if I might have had the nerve to perform such an act if it were daylight. A sensible part of me seems to whisper that what I did should be commended, since I've blessed the old woman with an eternal salvation she would have otherwise never located until it was far too late. However, there's a smaller, quieter, insidious part of my mind that whispers obscenities and tells me that I'm a monster for doing something so vile, so unreservedly wicked.

The word *murder* never really enters my mind. In a way, I've helped her. I've carried her across the threshold and delivered her to the painlessness of a godless oblivion. Of course, she won't be reunited with her daughter, as she probably hoped. None of us will eventually find loved ones, as we were promised in Sunday school. I know that to be true. Christianity has made sycophants of most of us—lobotomized zombies who will suckle at any available teat even if it's leaking lighter fluid and we're holding a torch.

It's exceptionally humorous how Christianity often condemns things that openly embrace the art form of magic, the espousal of the absurd, the advocacy of the farcical, considering how senselessly its sacred literature conveys its alleged truth. I imagine there are still nuns lobbying for the elimination of *Frosty the Snowman* reruns because of its shameless promotion of magic. It's absurdly comical when you consider how prominently pagan practices figure in the foundation of the supposedly holy text. The Christian Bible is nothing more than a book of fairy tales written by clerics and other so-called holy men who might have found success today in the art form of speculative fiction.

I wonder if guilt will ever trickle into my mind, if I might one day become burdened with grief, with the knowledge that I have taken a life. But this was a victory.

I have done more for that poor, pathetic creature than a lifetime of self-help audiotapes could have ever done. She would have never done it on her own. There was obviously a secret part of her that still wanted to live, wanted to thrive and be told that life is a grand and wondrous thing to behold. That was a foolish notion on her part. It was a gross misjudgment on my part to perpetuate the myth that life is worth living to people who are so delicate, so fragile, that they might split apart like wet straw at any given moment.

It's then that I wonder how I can best continue on this path and help others in the same way. I've spent too many months lying to my clients, willing them to abandon their suicidal ideation and embrace the rotten prospect of surviving tumultuous hardship.

At dark, I become loathsome.

I'll need to continue performing these rituals at night. If it were daylight when I first encountered the old woman, I might have had more reservations. I might have paled when I saw her in the hot afternoon sun, might have thought she possessed the same grace, the same elegance, of my dear mother, who was taken from me at an age when a boy truly needs love and tenderness in his life. At least now I'm not saddled with a clear, perfect image of the old woman to consider when I'm feeling especially vulnerable. I only saw her under moonlight or by the use of my flashlight. Much of her face remains a mystery to me even now.

I think of the man I'm supposed to meet tomorrow

night and I can't help but wonder if I'll possess the same nerve I willed into existence tonight. Though I was able to perform the task on a sweet old woman, I already know I won't be immune to this man's charms. Still, there's a part of me that wonders if it will be an arduous ritual, if I'll break under the pressure or if I'll have second thoughts, secret longings to abandon the exercise entirely.

As I drive along the narrow dirt road, silhouettes of trees flickering in my rearview mirror, I can't help but think of something my father told me when I was little. He explained that every baby is born with a small worm attached to its brain—a tiny caterpillar the size of a thimble. He told me how the little worm gets scared when we're frightened, is furious when we're angry, is depressed when we're sad. My father said that sometimes the worm in our head perishes while we are still alive and we're left to our own devices. I think that happens when we lose somebody we truly love—the little worm coiled inside our brain withers away to nothing and we're left to process the grief, the heartache, the misery, all alone. I know for certain that's what happened to me when I lost Pema and Bailey—the worm expired and left me on my own.

At dark, I become loathsome.

I arrive home about half an hour later and kick off my shoes as I scrape the dirt from them on the doorstep. I peer around the dimly lit living room and notice that in my absentmindedness I left the TV on, a bright silver glow rinsing the walls while the television plays a muted black-and-white horror film from the 1960s. Dropping my keys in the small bowl on the credenza beside the front door, I search for the remote. Finally, I uncover it buried beneath a half-eaten bag of peanuts on the coffee table. I aim the remote at the TV and all light is vacuumed from the screen in an instant.

I sit on the couch and fumble at the lamp for the switch. Twisting it on, I notice the lamp's reflection appear, a bright dot, in the center of the TV screen's dark mirror. I can't help but notice how something seems to stir in the reflection, beside the lamp, in the dim space where two walls meet. My eyes narrow to slits as I squint. It's then that I notice Pema's dark silhouette, reflected in the TV screen. Her face is a black void where all light seems to disappear, an empty pit where sound and reason go to die. Though she's obscured by the darkness that seems to ripple like a lake's surface, I can make out her bald head, like a monk's sacred tonsure.

"You're home late," she says to me.

I think of lighting a cigarette. After all, I've earned it.

"This one was . . . arduous," I tell her. "I wasn't sure if it would ever end. I wasn't even sure *how* it would end."

"It ended differently than the others," she says, crossing her arms.

I gaze at her reflection, silently begging her to come closer and step toward the light where I can see her properly. She doesn't, always so willfully obstinate to what I want and need even in her death.

"How do you know that?" I ask her.

"You think I don't see what you do?"

I swipe a pack of cigarettes from the table and light one. I inhale deeply.

"It was perfect, wasn't it?" I ask her. "That poor woman. Her suffering is over because of me."

Pema looks at me with visible distress.

"Or perhaps it's just started," she says.

I tap the end of the cigarette in the silver ashtray Pema's father gifted to me one Christmas long ago, when Pema and I were first married. It's one of the few relics I keep of the fleeting friendship her father and I once shared. He won't return my calls anymore, no matter how many times I attempt to contact him.

"What do you mean by that?" I ask.

"She's going to be alive in that coffin until she suffocates," Pema tells me. "Alone. Frightened."

I shake my head. I know exactly what Pema's trying to do—how she's attempting to mutate and malform the success of my victory in my mind.

"Only for a few minutes," I tell her. "Would you have her carry on like that for years? Alone? Frightened?"

"She came to you because she wanted to live," Pema reminds me. "She didn't want to die."

"She didn't know she wanted to die," I say. "Too stupid to realize it. I've done her the ultimate kindness. I've ended her suffering. Called off her misery."

Pema laughs, genuinely amused. Her laugh sounds thin, almost metallic, as if there were electrical cords in her throat.

"You know what your problem is, Ashley?"

I don't respond. I know she's going to tell me even without my asking.

"You're a skilled artisan when it comes to completing artistic works that you can't undo," Pema tells me. "Things that you can't unmake—ever."

I shake my head. "I don't know what you mean."

"Think of the way you killed that old woman tonight as if it were a charcoal drawing on parchment," she says.

I leap out of my chair. "I did not kill her."

"You'd be the only artist in the world whose artwork

wouldn't burn," she says. "The things you create, you can't take back."

My gaze lowers until I'm staring at my shoes, avoiding her reflection at all costs. "Perhaps I don't want to."

"Even the thing you said to your son?" she asks me.

It's then I begin to sense my cheeks growing heated. I feel my tongue swelling, throat getting dryer, and it's suddenly difficult to breathe.

"He didn't hear me," I tell her. "He didn't hear what I said."

In my peripheral vision, I notice her reflection drawing closer to me. She glides across the floor as if she were suspended from the ceiling by cables.

"You're certain of that?" she asks me. "You're willing to continue believing that?"

Perhaps once I was. But not any longer.

"I never meant to hurt him," I say. "I should have never done what I did."

That was true. I should have never done what I did to Bailey. But that's why it's more important than ever to find him and bring him home and be the loving father I should have always been to him—the father he always deserved.

"You think he'll ever forgive you?" Pema asks.

She doesn't seem to be attempting to stoke the embers of the guilt I've been fanning to flames for months now. Rather, she seems to be genuinely curious, wondering if I truly know my son.

"I have to find him," is my response. "I'll never know if I don't."

"The police think he's dead," she says. "You saw the hat they found."

My eyes narrow at her for a moment. "Wouldn't you know by now if he was?"

"It doesn't work that way," Pema replies. "You think he's still out there?"

My attention begins to drift away from Pema, pulled toward the glow of the lamp flickering against the wall beside me.

"I don't know anymore," I say. "But I want to believe there's some good left in the world. Just like what I'm doing to help people."

Pema laughs again. "You're not helping people. You're murdering them."

I turn my head to look at Pema, but the doorframe is empty and my wife is gone. There's a lingering firmness in the air—something unspoken that wants to be said, something that wants to tell me that Pema no longer loves me as she once did because she now sees me differently. It's a surprise to realize that I do not mourn the idea of her love vanishing, spiraling down an invisible drain, a gutter that we built together. If she considers me to be a monster, so be it.

I slip outside onto the back porch and gaze up at a sky so endless and so devastatingly black that it could swallow me whole if it had the will to do so. As I take another drag from my cigarette, I think of the small worm my father told me about, lying wilted and bloodless in the furthest recesses of my mind—a helpless, pathetic thing that expired when I lost Bailey and now lies there stinking like beached carrion. I think of poking the dead creature until it explodes and then squeezing its precious innards across my brain as if I were applying watercolors to a blank canvas. I am, after all, a creator, a true architect; what I make, no matter what, cannot be unmade.

Yet, after all, even in my darkest and most hopeless moments, there's a particular thought I desperately hold on to: Worms usually lay eggs.

—

At dark, I become loathsome.

For some inexplicable reason, my mind returns to the young man I agreed to meet the next day—the one with the velvety smooth voice, the one my father would have loved. I concede that there's jealousy lingering there, a considerable amount of envy that he could be so masculine, so decidedly rough around the edges. The two of us would be like sticks of kindling rubbing together. The world would burn brightly around us.

I think of killing him.

I think of hurting him in such a way that he'll never be able to recover. The thoughts excite me. It brings me glee to think of the ways in which I could dispatch this poor, unsuspecting soul.

At dark, I become loathsome.

I think of calling him again, just to hear the sound of his voice. I think of keeping him on the phone and unzipping my jeans while he talks. I think of stroking myself until I'm completely firm—working my hands up and down, rubbing my cock until I can bear the pressure no longer.

But I don't. I decide not to do any of that. I'd be too angry with myself for indulging in a fantasy of a man I hardly know—a man I cannot help but envy. A man I plan to kill.

At dark, I become loathsome.

There's a part of me that wants to know his name.

I know I shouldn't. It's not part of the ritual. But some quiet, undisturbed part of me is aching to know his name. After all, when you know someone's name, they belong to you in a certain intimate way. You can call upon them and they will come to you.

I think of waiting outside my house for him. I think of spouting names into the night and waiting for someone to answer.

At dark, I become loathsome.

I think of the revolting story about Keane Withers that the man told me in our private chat. It felt strange to read what he had written. How much it excited me!

Every horror story is about power. Whether it's blatantly displayed or more discreet, every horror story is about power. The story the young man told me was certainly no exception.

At dark, I become loathsome.

One of my own rules when performing these rituals is that they are never to be performed so close together. But I can't bear the thought of canceling the meeting with masterjinx76. There's something inexplicable pulling me toward him. I wonder what other dark secrets he might be willing to share. There's something about his presence, online and over the phone, that I can't help but become completely enchanted by.

There's something dangerous about him. It's almost as if he possesses a dark secret that only I can drag out of him.

CHAPTER NINE

The following morning, the moment I wake up, I realize it's a day I've been dreading: Bailey's birthday. The horrible reminder hits me even as I wipe the crust from my eyes.

I could stay in bed.

Or I could keep moving.

Something compels me to crawl out of bed and make my way into the bathroom.

To distract myself, I think about tonight's ritual. I realize I could try to coerce the poor, unsuspecting fool into the grave I dig and cover his body with a plastic tarp so that he's clean from dirt, but there's something more appealing about the idea of loading him into a proper coffin. I have to somehow get my hands on a new coffin.

I take a shower and get dressed, then head downstairs

and grab an apple from the small bowl of fruit on the kitchen counter. I wince as I bite down on a soggy mass; sour juice trickles across my mouth and smears my chin. Spitting the bite into the sink, I look at the apple and find the center of the fruit is spoiled—the apple's core shining black as onyx, rotted. I toss the apple into the trash and down a swig of water from a nearby pitcher.

When I'm finished scrubbing the bitter taste from my mouth with a washcloth, I snatch my keys from the credenza and dash out to the garage. I close the door behind me and circle the van, then open the vehicle's door and lift myself into the driver's seat. As I twist the keys in my hand, one of the sharp ends pushes into my skin as if it were a small penance, a minor reparation for what I did last night—the innocent human life I obliterated from the world. I still feel no guilt for the life I ended. It's not that I despised her or wished her unwell. I merely wanted to set her free.

And I have.

I've done everything possible to see that her suffering has ended. What more could I have done?

As I think of the old woman I buried alive last night, my mind begins to wander to other, more pernicious thoughts—thoughts of the futility of my existence and the very possible likelihood that Bailey has perished. I remember how easy it was, after Pema passed away, for me to steal away to the garage, close all the doors and windows, shove the keys into the ignition, and sit in a corner while fumes filled the small space. I sit there, twisting the keys farther and farther into my skin, trying to recall what stopped me from going through with it. I struggle to remember what motivated me to pull the keys from the ignition and stagger from the garage in a blind panic, choking on fumes and tirelessly swatting the air.

It's then I recall how the keys somehow seemed to hurl themselves from the ignition on their own as if an invisible hand had dragged them out in a foolish endeavor to keep me alive, to deny me the sweet release of death.

Why should I deny myself any longer? Is it truly my vocation to end the suffering of others, or should I be more concerned with my own despair? I couldn't possibly save all the souls that need my help, that need to be released from their misery and anguish.

It's all quite pointless now.

None of it really matters. It never did. I tricked myself into believing that it mattered so that I could carry on and pass through life on a gentle current, the same way a branch does when it falls into a river and is eventually carried out toward emerald seawater. But that's no way to live. That's no way to exist—the unbearable monotony of each day, drifting on a current that you cannot control, time passing all around you in a blur while you stay very much the same. If I were a branch that had been tossed into a river, I would gladly sink to the bottom.

What's the point of pretending that we're being carried through the universe by the giant hand of some caring, compassionate deity?

We're not, and there is no point.

The worm that tickles our brain shrivels and dies, and before long it's our time to expire as well.

Pema's parents don't talk to me anymore, as if I've been marked *Dangerous. Do not touch.* I'd probably be able to stomach their abandonment more if my parents were still alive.

At a twinge of pain, I look down and realize I've twisted the key into the center of my hand. Blood as black as ink is filling the small bowl of my open palm. I pull the key out of the hole I've opened in my flesh.

Do I dare? I wonder, looking from the bloody key to the van's ignition. *Do I dare shove the key in there and twist it? All this pointless suffering would go away.*

Yes. I wouldn't be reminded of my heartache, my misery, my despair, day in and day out. I wouldn't be a neutered, thoughtless prisoner on a gentle current that seems to only carry me back and forth, from one woeful bank of the river to the other.

As I'm about to push the key into the ignition, a small silhouette comes into view outside the driver's window.

I can sense my eyes widening at the sight.

"Bailey—?"

"You still have to find me," he says.

I swallow hard, the muscles in my throat as immovable as bedrock. "They think you're gone for good."

"Is that what you think?" my son asks.

I sense tears beading in the corners of my eyes. "I don't know what to think anymore."

"You always gave up on me," Bailey says, his eyes lowering as he turns away from me. "Even on my birthday."

"That's not true," I tell him. "I want to believe you're still out there. I want to believe I can still find you."

"Sometimes it's easier not to believe," he says gently, beginning to withdraw back into the dark.

"Where are you going?" I ask, straightening.

"You still have to find me," he says, just before he disappears.

I sit there for a few moments, listening to the sound of my heartbeat hammering away in the space between my ears.

I could have ended it all. But something stopped me—the notion that Bailey might still be alive, that he might be out there, waiting for me. I can't abandon him, as I did before. He deserves a better father than that. It's then I realize that it's probably in my best interest to stay the course and commit to what I decided earlier—to save the poor souls of those who are afflicted, who are suffering. After all, it's what they deserve and, more importantly, what they've earned, after so many years of hopelessness.

My first step is clear: I must visit the mortician a few towns over and inquire about the possibility of him selling me another coffin.

I get out of the van and leave the garage, heading into the house to grab a bandage.

—

After I finish dressing the wound in the center of my palm, I amble outside and head for the garage again. I climb into the driver's seat, turn on the ignition, and thumb the button to open the garage door. The door lifts, rattling like a snake's tail.

I shift into Reverse and sail out of the garage, retreating into the empty street and then motoring along the narrow lane lined with other small houses—homes filled with people I once knew, people who stopped coming by after Pema and Bailey were gone, the hopelessness of my grief some terrible illness that they could contract at any moment.

That's something I think about often: how people around you change when you lose a loved one. The manner in which they refer to you, the gentler way in which they approach you as if you might rip apart under the slightest pressure. Their courteousness comes from a place of goodwill and sympathy; however, it only reaffirms the fact that you're different, that you're marked with something irreversible, that you're only as decent as unusable goods.

That's what I am to some people. That's how they think of me—unusable goods.

As I drive, I think of some of the families in the neighborhood that used to come around often. They'd stay for dinner or ask if Bailey could go to their house to play with their children. I think of how some of the wives in the neighborhood brought warm dinners for us when Pema was going through chemotherapy, their kindness when Bailey was especially frightened he might forever lose his mother. I would always comfort him and assure him that I would do everything I could to

love him and care for him, but my promises did little to calm him.

After all, he knew full well what kind of father I was—distant, uncaring, far more concerned with shoving ornate pieces of metal into parts of his face than coping with his wife's untimely demise.

I begin to think how those same families stopped visiting after a while, as if afraid that my grief might somehow infect them, might somehow contaminate their precious lives. I think of how it wasn't long before I was considered a monster in Henley's Edge—a creature undeserving of sympathy or even a semblance of compassion. The gentle way neighbors and loved ones approached me began to firm with bitterness or, even worse, loathing, as I drastically altered my appearance out of misery. At first, I had the piercings done to cope with the heartache, the pain of losing my beloved Pema. But it soon became something of a challenge—a way to defy all those who pitied me or thought me unnatural because I wasn't grieving the way they thought I should. That's a thing people don't talk about enough—that there are people who will judge even the way you mourn your loved ones.

My drive will take me to the one person in the state of Connecticut who hasn't judged me unfairly or held me in contempt: Norman Restarick of Restarick & Sons Funeral Home in the quiet town of Salisbury. Mr. Restarick was so caring and devoted when we interred Pema.

I still can't bring myself to refer to him by his first name. It would be too disrespectful, too discourteous, given his sophisticated nature. He's probably the only mortician in the world who plays iconic performances from La Scala Opera House in Milan, Italy, on the small television set arranged in the entryway.

Finally, after half an hour or so, I arrive at the funeral home, a prominent building on the town's main street. The small Dutch Colonial has been remodeled somewhat, expanded from its original size. I steer my van into the driveway and pull into the building's rear parking lot, leaving the vehicle stationed beneath an old oak. I'd expected the tree would have come down two summers ago when a tornado ripped through the northwest corner of our state like a giant beast's claw, yet there it still stands. I amble around the front of the building, climb the front steps, and stop outside the front door, which is decorated with a handsome wreath of begonias.

I knock twice and wait.

After a second or two, the door opens, and the diminutive frame of Mr. Restarick fills the doorway. The year since I last saw him has not been kind. His face is pock-marked and sun-wizened like a raisin. His spine is so visibly arched that it appears as if an invisible clothing hanger remains tucked inside his white dress shirt. His hair is ice white and dramatically swirled, resembling the thin twigs of a bird's nest.

"My dear boy," he says, ushering me across the threshold and into the foyer. "I was hoping you'd stop by again one of these days. You've been in trouble," he adds, looking at me closely.

"Maybe a little," I say, forcing the politest smile I can conjure as he shuts the door behind me.

"No Victoria today?" I ask, noticing that the small reception area is empty.

"I sent her home early," Restarick says. "Her nephew won a regional spelling bee and this afternoon he's competing in the statewide contest in Hartford. She told me she'd call and let me know how he does."

"I don't want to keep you," I tell him.

"Nonsense," Restarick says. "You're very welcome."

"How are you feeling?" I ask as he leads me down the narrow hallway toward his office in the rear of the building. "I heard you had your gallbladder out last year."

"Some days are better than others," he responds, gesturing to the small chair in the corner of his office.

"Mornings are the most difficult usually. Arthritis. Doctor insists I'm healthy."

"He would know."

"Maybe," Restarick says, easing into a chair and exhaling as he finds a comfortable spot. "I make a poor patient, I'm afraid."

"You look well," I say, though that's not true.

I wonder if he can tell I'm lying. Despite his age, he's sharper than most expect. After all, he's still working in his early eighties.

I shrink a little as he leans forward in his chair, eyes narrowing to slits.

"You certainly didn't come all this way to discuss my health," he says. "What's on your mind?"

I fidget, stirring in my seat nervously. "You remember that coffin you sold me a while back?"

"Beautiful model," he says, eyes closing as if recalling the fineness of such craftsmanship. "You won't find boxes built like that outside of Sicily these days."

I inhale sharply, unsure how to say what I need to say.

"I'm afraid I need another one," I tell him.

Restarick looks at me queerly. "Another one? Has there been—?"

"Nothing's wrong," I assure him.

Restarick glances away and gently rubs his forehead,

clearly unsettled. At last he looks directly at me again. "I never asked what you needed the first one for. You insisted that it was a private matter and I respected that. But now, I wonder . . ."

I bite my lip.

"What are you doing with these coffins?" he continues. "It's not something I'm . . . *concerned* about, but I am curious. You'll have to humor an old man." From the firmness of his gaze, I can tell that he won't give me the coffin if I don't give him some kind of answer.

"I can pay more," I promise him. "I can give you more than I gave you the last time."

The old man shakes his head, his mouth wrinkling like a scar. "The money is unimportant. My curiosity needs to be fed, dear boy."

He looks at me, expecting me to say something, to perhaps offer up a confession as if he were a holy man. When I don't respond, he appears somewhat vexed.

"What could you possibly be doing with these items?" he asks me.

I stand up and move over to the window overlooking the small garden behind the house and near the parking lot. I think for a moment, wondering what I could tell him that would satisfy his curiosity without giving myself away entirely. I rehearsed something during my drive, but now the excuse seems trite and meaningless. In a matter of seconds, I think of something else.

"I hold funerals," I say, turning to face him.

Restarick's eyebrows furrow, face scrunching.

"I hold little ceremonies to put my son to rest," I continue. "I held the first one a while ago, using the coffin you sold me. It kept the bad thoughts away for months. I was doing fine. I had come to terms with everything, I thought. But lately, things have been growing more and more difficult. I wonder if it'll ever get easier."

The old man's face thaws, visibly softening.

"I need to hold another ceremony for my boy," I say. "It's his birthday today, you know? It may not make sense to you, but it makes sense to me."

Restarick is quiet for some time, regarding me with more than a little bewilderment. Finally, he nods and speaks:

"Yes, I quite understand. It's hard to put to rest those we love when we're not certain where they are or what they've become."

"It helps me grieve," I add.

"You've given up all hope?"

I hesitate a little. "I'm . . . not sure. I only know what works for me."

My apparent abject misery seems to have reached him.

"Anything you need," he says, then pauses. "I don't have any children's coffins available at the moment. You'll have to make do with an adult model."

"That's fine," I reply. It's what I want anyway. Plenty of room for tonight's client.

"You'll have to carry it yourself," the old man says. "With nothing on the calendar for this afternoon, I let my assistants leave as well as Victoria."

"How much?" I ask.

Restarick considers, then says, "I'm afraid any price would be unreasonable. I just ask that you take care of yourself, dear boy."

—

After I haul the coffin from the cellar and drag it out to my van, Restarick escorts me to the front porch of the house to say goodbye.

"I can't thank you enough for your kindness," I say, squeezing both of his hands tight.

His hands feel weak, cold. His skin leathery like ancient parchment.

"It's not kindness," he says. "It's the proper thing to do."

Just before I step away, he taps me on the shoulder and grabs hold of me.

"Remember what I said?" he asks. "Take care of yourself. Sometimes it's easy to lose ourselves in despair and heartache. When those moments come, a trick I've learned is to repeat my name again and again. Understand?"

I nod slowly.

"That way, you'll always remember who you are," he tells me. "Don't forget who you are, dear boy. That would be a real tragedy."

After a final squeeze, our hands part and I head for my van, waving at Restarick as I make my way along the narrow driveway.

For now, I have obtained what I need. Of course, after tonight's ritual, I'll need to go through the taxing exercise of locating another coffin for the next one and another for the one after that. But since I have nothing scheduled after tonight, this is something to be considered at a later date. What matters most now is that the coffin has been secured without any financial outlay, and I will be able to complete my new ritual tonight, on Bailey's birthday.

I climb into the driver's seat and pull out of the funeral home's driveway. I find myself sailing down the street, beckoned by some unknown, indefinite force—something that calls to me, murmuring my name over and over again.

Hearing the echo makes me realize that I'm repeating my name again and again under my breath, whispering softly to myself, *Ashley, Ashley, Ashley* . . .

CHAPTER TEN

At dark, I become loathsome.

Other than the hope of one day finding Bailey and finally being the father he always deserved, there's one reason in particular why it's been a struggle to kill myself—why I continue to hesitate and why I always falter when the inviting opportunity is there in front of me. It's a story I read online about a young man named Tandy with a peculiar appetite for illness, disease, and infection. It's a story I've memorized the same way a child might obsess over a favorite picture book at bedtime. Very often it's the only thing I can think about . . .

—

THE ORDEAL OF VICTOR AND TANDY

Tandy was thirty-seven years old when he realized his husband's cancer diagnosis turned him on.

This horrible realization made him yearn for the days when he contemplated the demise of both of his parents. He could still recall the moment when he first realized he wished his loved ones unwell. It was midafternoon on a Saturday in July and his parents were watching a news program about a mentally disturbed teenager who had pilfered a knife from the kitchen drawer, crept into his parents' room, and butchered them while they slept. Tandy recalled considering how simple it would be for him to do the same—to steal some of the fine, unwashed cutlery from the kitchen sink and give his parents a nightmare from which they would never awaken.

Naturally, Tandy was surprised to find himself contemplating something so ghoulish, so unequivocally ghastly. He became upset with himself, looking inward in desperate search of the poisonous root that had evidently made its home deep inside him, in some subterranean grotto where logic or reason could not follow.

He thought he was a monster.

Perhaps he was.

Something excited him about the idea of being the cause of someone else's suffering, someone else's despair, someone else's wish to die.

That night in July, Tandy asked his parents to drive him to the emergency room, thinking there was something wrong with him. After all, what normal nineteen-year-old fantasizes about slaughtering their parents? The medical staff at the hospital didn't seem to think anything was wrong with him, but then again, you can't see the ugliness of a person's thoughts in an x-ray. Instead of real help, he was prescribed a cocktail of antidepressants that he took for the next five years.

It turned out that was just his first horrible fixation.

Tandy never expected to find satisfaction, pleasure—even a semblance of perverted amusement—in something as decidedly offensive as a serious illness. More importantly, he never intended to tell his husband, Victor, how much he delighted in Victor's suffering, how he became aroused when he noticed Victor's body curling in on itself like an insect in the cold, how he worshipped Victor when his hair began to fall out because of the radiation treatment.

Victor didn't need to know of his husband's perversion. Though perhaps he suspected something was amiss when their sex life became much more active after his diagnosis. That was the moment everything had changed for Tandy, just as it had changed for Victor. Just as he can recall the moment when he considered the harm he could reasonably do to his parents, Tandy can recall the moment when his fixation on his husband's cancer began: a rainy, cold Wednesday morning in March.

They had visited the local emergency care facility because Victor had complained of abdominal pain for a few days. Their concern had grown considerably that morning, since when Victor woke up and went to the bathroom, he found the toilet bowl filled with bright red blood.

It hadn't been long before they received the news: a tumor resting on the lower part of his colon.

Victor buried his face in his hands, sobbing quietly, as the doctor continued to explain the seriousness of his conclusion. Tandy was only half listening, his mind immediately beginning to fruit with endless possibilities of sexual pleasures he had never considered before. He imagined slamming himself into the warmth of Victor's entrails, moving inside his guts, maybe even feeling the polyp as he stirred there. He sensed himself becoming hard, the crotch of his pants shortening as he sat beside his beloved husband in the small hospital room.

Tandy found himself surprised at his own thoughts, yet there was a quiet, secret part of him that reveled in them, that basked in the grotesquerie he had already built within his mind. He imagined Victor becoming something truly repugnant. When Victor finally matured to his final form—his last form before death inevitably claimed him—that's when Tandy figured he would truly savor his husband's body. Perhaps even after.

He could imagine the headlines: *Social Worker Keeps Remains of Cancer Victim in House for Weeks After Death.*

Although he was disgusted with himself for thinking something so abominable, it wasn't as if he could reach into his brain and turn the faucet off. Medication can sometimes reduce the flow of horrible thoughts—medication Tandy no longer took—but little can be done to shut them down completely. Sometimes, the more you resist them, the more powerful they become.

Tandy realized when he was very young that there were only two reasons to fully love somebody. The first reason was lust—an indescribable ache to fully possess someone and make them belong to you in a way that they'd never belong to another human being. The second reason was respect—a tender, more compassionate reason to mate with a partner and call them yours.

Although he had originally fallen in love with Victor because he respected him—venerated him, even—Tandy realized that that respect had dimmed considerably and given way to an uncontrollable lust. He wanted to possess Victor, and all of Victor, or he might splinter apart. Even in Tandy's delirium, he knew he was being overly dramatic. He knew he was smitten with the operatic nature of love or death.

As they drove home from the hospital, Tandy invented countless scenarios that both entertained and frightened him. Tandy wondered what Victor might say if he told him of these new feelings, if he confessed to his husband how much he loved him and the new reason why. Tandy figured that Victor might shrink in disgust and refer to him as a monster. Tandy wondered how it might feel for his feet to slam on the gas while he steered their little car toward a thicket of trees beside the roadway.

They'd be dead then, both of them: their crumpled bodies thrown against the cracked windshield like sheets of tattered newspapers. Perhaps Tandy was better off dead. Perhaps they both were. The very least he could do for his mental indiscretions was to put his beloved Victor out of his misery, to end his suffering. If he did that, would Tandy somehow be absolved of his transgressions, his moments of impropriety? After all, was there anything that could be done to save Victor? Of course, the doctor had seemed somewhat hopeful about Victor's prognosis, but there was something grim about the way he had delivered the news of the possible surgery—the corners of his mouth pulling down and his eyes lowering.

Victor had been grim, too, and despondent. His responses to the doctor vibrated with indecision. There was something lovely about his hesitation, something truly wondrous about how he showed his discomfort. Tandy savored those precious moments of agony.

They didn't talk much when they finally returned home. Tandy offered to reheat some of the leftovers they had in the fridge, but Victor said he wasn't hungry. His appetite had recently waned considerably, and while Tandy pitied him, there was something enticing about the thought of him wasting away, his once-healthy form shrinking until he was as emaciated as a Holocaust survivor. Once again, Tandy found pleasure in such vile thoughts—fancying his beloved Victor coming to resemble nothing more than a walking corpse, a skeletal embodiment of the fragility of human life. Victor didn't deserve this. Any of this. At least Tandy was able to recognize that sad fact. It wasn't that he wished Victor unwell, but rather that Tandy wished him to surrender to the inevitability of his illness. Tandy knew Victor was fighting for his life, but the regrettable truth was that Tandy was waiting for Victor's sickness to win.

Since Victor wasn't hungry, Tandy asked if he wanted to sit and watch television, as they always did late at night. Reruns of classic shows that their parents used to watch, like *I Love Lucy* or *Green Acres.* But Victor wasn't interested. Instead, he said he was going to draw a bath and soak for an hour or so before bed. Tandy offered to help prepare the bathtub and suggested using some of the rose petals from the lovely bouquet Victor's mother had sent them a few days earlier, but Victor said he preferred to do it on his own.

Tandy could tell that the thought of surgery was weighing heavily on Victor's mind. Why wouldn't it? After all, Victor had been a specimen of health for most of his life, especially during the time that Tandy had known him. It must have been like entering a nightmare world to be suddenly whisked away to hospitals where doctors and nurses poked and prodded him.

After Tandy waited a few hours, he crept upstairs to find Victor. The bathtub was empty. Instead, Victor was in the main bedroom, reclining in the bed and pretending to read a book he had bought nearly two summers earlier when they'd visited Martha's Vineyard. It was unusual behavior; Victor wasn't the type to spend his free time reading a book that resembled the kind of surrealist trash he mocked whenever they visited bookstores or went to the movies.

Entering the room, Tandy made some teasing comment, but his husband didn't even glance up, just pretended Tandy wasn't even there. Even in his sullenness, Tandy found him attractive. He couldn't help but imagine more disease fruiting inside Victor, little polyps blossoming in his darkest, most precious places.

"I'll sleep on the couch tonight," Victor said, tearing the sheets away and tossing his legs over the side of the bed.

Tandy leaned against him, pushing him back down. "What's wrong? Tell me."

"Nothing."

Tandy gave him a look. He knew something was upsetting Victor. Of course, he was also certain that he knew what that was, but he wanted Victor to tell him.

"I'm . . . scared," Victor whispered as he lowered his eyes.

Tandy expected Victor to express his fear through sobbing and uncontrollable pleas to a deity to cure him of his ailment. He hadn't expected this composure. Tandy admired his husband's willingness to remain calm despite the fear. He couldn't help but wonder what he would be like if he were the one with such a horrible diagnosis, if he had been marked with the same incurable disease.

Sitting beside Victor on the bed, Tandy wrapped an arm around his beloved and pulled him tight against his body.

"The surgery?" he asked.

Victor merely nodded.

Tandy couldn't blame Victor. There was nothing more excruciatingly painful than the thought of someone opening you up and reorganizing or removing a part of your insides. Even if those insides were spoiled, it certainly wasn't the kind of topic for polite dinner conversation, much less pillow talk.

As much as he loathed admitting it, this was an opportunity for Tandy to convince Victor not to go through with the operation. This was a chance to urge him to reconsider and, more importantly, prolong his illness.

Tandy detested himself for thinking something so vile, but the thoughts trickled more steadily once he gave in to them, quietly urging Tandy to convince Victor not to agree to the operation.

That would keep him sick. Moreover, that would keep him attractive in Tandy's eyes.

Even with the diagnosis so recent, Tandy already dreaded the moment when Victor would be cured, when the last bit of cancer would be scraped out and he would forever be referred to as "a survivor."

Tandy didn't want that for him. He wanted Victor to be his precious, disease-filled lover as long as his body could endure the affliction.

"Don't do it," Tandy said, that night.

Victor glanced at him quickly, surprised by his brashness.

"Don't?" he asked.

"I'm scared too," Tandy said, grabbing his husband's hand and sensing a little heartbeat between his fingers. "I just . . . don't want to lose you."

It wasn't that Tandy was lying. He meant every word. But he hated the thought of Victor recovering more than the thought of watching him deteriorate until he was practically unrecognizable. The prospect of Victor changing—transforming—excited Tandy. It filled him with a joy he had never sensed before, and he knew full well he would do anything to keep that joy close to him, to keep it from dying out.

Victor looked surprised, his eyebrows furrowing. "I just—I thought you were going to talk me into it. I thought that would be what you wanted."

Tandy feigned a polite smile, pulling Victor tighter against him until the sick man's shoulder was buried in his armpit. "I want you to be safe. I want things to get better for you. But I'm not convinced surgery is the answer."

Victor looked deep in thought, staring off into the distance.

"I thought you'd tell me everything would be fine," he said.

"Do you want me to lie to you?"

Whether Victor was impressed with his brashness or annoyed, Tandy couldn't be certain. Victor often put his emotions on full display, but lately he had been quartered off as if hiding something, seemingly distrustful of anything and everything. Why shouldn't he be? His own body had betrayed him and in one of the worst ways possible.

"You don't think I should go through with it?" Victor asked.

Tandy shook his head, looking steadily at his husband to stress the seriousness of what he believed. Victor had to believe what Tandy said was true.

"There are other ways to fight this," Tandy told him. "Other treatments. Healthier options."

Victor still didn't look convinced. His lips moved silently, struggling to say something he knew he couldn't.

"We'll check them out tomorrow," Tandy offered, pecking Victor's forehead with a kiss.

Finally, Victor leaned into Tandy's embrace, his little body softening in surrender.

Without hesitation, Tandy pulled off Victor's underwear and spread him out on the bed before servicing him. It wasn't long before Victor's dick filled Tandy's mouth with warm fluid. Then Tandy was only too delighted to flip Victor over, exposing his hairless buttocks, and push himself deep inside the other man until he completely disappeared.

That's what Tandy yearned for most of all—to disappear inside Victor, to crawl into him and build a little nest. A place where he could be safe, where he could love the things he loved about Victor without shame or embarrassment. Tandy supposed that's what most lovemaking sessions between two lovers felt like—like trying to crawl into one another and make their body your home.

After they were finished, Tandy watched Victor roll onto his side to sleep. He looked so peaceful, so delicate and decidedly fragile. Nobody could have guessed there was something vile flowering inside him.

It was strange to think how desperately Tandy wanted the root of Victor's cancer to survive, as though another person were dwelling inside him. Of course, it scared Tandy to think of losing Victor completely—to watch him wither away and expire—but it frightened him even more to think of going a day without Victor's illness nearby, accessible for his pleasure.

Tandy detested himself for thinking it, but he yearned for a way to keep both Victor and his precious illness alive. Of course, Tandy knew one would destroy the other before long, but he couldn't help but wonder if there was a way to possess Victor forever, to keep his exquisite disease.

There were times when Tandy truly wondered if he was capable of hurting someone, if he had unwittingly been endowed with the same monstrous tendencies as others who torture, maim, and kill just for the sheer satisfaction.

After all, what Tandy had done to Victor was inexcusable, was a kind of violence. He had convinced his husband, the man he supposedly loved, not to have surgery because of Tandy's own predilections, his own perversions. Tandy wanted to keep Victor sick, and he knew Victor would stay sick as long as Tandy was the voice of reason in his life. Victor had a small circle of friends and his relationship with his parents was somewhat strained, to say the least.

Victor and Tandy cared for one another and invented their own family, the way many other queer people create a chosen family.

Theoretically, Tandy knew he could persuade Victor to do anything and convince him it was for the best. He knew for a fact that Victor trusted him. He had put his faith in Tandy completely and thought Tandy would never do anything to hurt him. That was what pulled on Tandy's conscience the most—Victor's unwavering trust. Tandy dreaded the day when Victor would realize he was a monster, the day Victor would realize that his husband could indeed hurt him and that, even worse, Tandy had systematically been doing so ever since his diagnosis.

To say that things were pleasant between Victor and Tandy for the next few days was an understatement.

Tandy pampered Victor with flowers, imported chocolates, and other foods he adored but always lamented he could never eat for fear of gaining weight. They sneaked away from their work-from-home duties for sex at least twice a day. Sometimes three times, if they were feeling particularly inspired to ravish one another. Their intimate sessions weren't usually the lovemaking they had once enjoyed, but rather animalistic fucking. Tandy couldn't help but wonder if he was fucking Victor or if he was fucking the cancer Victor carried inside him. After all, it only took one thought of the lesions defiling his colon and Tandy was ready to mate.

After a week or so, Tandy noticed Victor becoming more and more lethargic; his participation in their lovemaking was half-hearted at best. More often he would complain it hurt too much and would insist on quick hand jobs to finish the matter. A light within him had dimmed nearly completely and was threatening to go out.

One afternoon, Tandy offered to step out to the store because they needed bleach for the pile of laundry they had neglected for a week now. Victor barely mumbled a farewell as Tandy left, and Tandy figured he was going through one of his occasional, but increasingly frequent, bouts of melancholy. When Tandy returned home, he found Victor sprawled out on the kitchen floor, a dark shadow of blood creeping across the tiles from where he had hit his head. If Tandy hesitated for a moment, it was due to shock, not because he wanted to revel in his husband's misfortune. Tandy dragged the phone from his pocket and dialed 911.

Victor drifted in and out of consciousness as they waited for the ambulance. Tandy cradled Victor in his arms, sobbing. Tandy had done this to him, Tandy and no one else. Tandy knew in his heart that this was because he had encouraged Victor to not go through with the surgery. His body was slowly breaking down and it was all Tandy's fault. The illness inside him—the precious thing Tandy cared for more than he cared for the man—was claiming him, inch by inch, until Victor would be able to do nothing but fully surrender.

Carrying a small bouquet of roses, Tandy crept into Victor's hospital room and found him lying in bed. Victor's eyes were closed, hands folded across his chest like a pharaoh about to be embalmed. He almost resembled a sleeping child, precious and helpless. An assortment of monitors and machines flanked his bedside; there were IVs in both arms and a tube snaked into one of his nostrils. Seeing this, Tandy cursed himself for wishing him unwell.

Tandy approached Victor cautiously, fearful to disturb him. Tandy had always been uneasy around sleeping people—not because they frightened him, but because they made him wonder what he might do to them if he had the chance. Tandy worried for the sleepers when he was near. What was to stop Tandy from bashing Victor over the head with the vase of flowers, then twisting bits of broken glass into his eyes?

As soon as Tandy set the vase down on his bedside table, Victor's eyelids fluttered open, and he blinked, wiping dampness from his eyes.

"Hey," Victor said, exhaling.

Tandy rubbed his fingers and cupped his hand.

Victor tried to straighten, but Tandy stopped him, urging him to rest. He obeyed without comment.

Tandy pulled a nearby chair to the bedside and sat, clasping Victor's hands.

"Remember the movie *Breakfast at Tiffany's*?"

Victor tilted his head, eyebrows furrowing.

"I know it's your favorite," Tandy continued. Victor nodded. "Remember what Holly Golightly says? She says, 'I'll never get used to anything. Anybody that does, they might as well be dead.' Remember?"

Victor still looked confused, mouth open slightly.

Tandy swallowed hard, feeling the muscles in his throat flexing. What was he trying to say? Was he finally going to confess why he had persuaded Victor to not have surgery? Was he going to out himself and throw himself at Victor's mercy? Tell Victor what he had been fantasizing about, how he had been using Victor for his illness, how the cancer had turned him on? It would devastate Victor. He would never trust Tandy again, and why should he? Tandy was a monster. Tandy had yearned to make a martyr out of Victor for his own sexual fulfillment. What was more monstrous than that?

"I guess—what I'm trying to say . . ." Tandy said, his voice trailing off for a moment. "I guess what I'm saying is I grew accustomed to how things were, and I didn't want to see things change. Even if it meant changing for the better."

Victor was quiet.

"I thought maybe if you had the surgery, you'd change," Tandy told him, lowering his eyes.

"They just want to help me," Victor said.

"Yes," Tandy said weakly. "They should help you."

Victor's eyes were shimmering with unshed tears.

"I have to go through with the surgery," Victor said,

his voice brittle and breaking. "If I don't, I'll die."

Tandy knew this was true.

He cursed himself for wanting to see Victor suffer, for wanting to see him languish in utter agony. Tandy had cared more for the cancer than he had for his husband. When would he finally be satisfied? When they were loading Victor's hairless body into a casket?

Tandy squeezed Victor's hand tightly, a silent apology the other man didn't even know he should have asked for.

Tandy knew things would be different after the surgery. Victor would heal and the cancer would be gone. Hopefully. But would Tandy love Victor less? He dreaded the thought. He even hated himself for dreading it—for detesting the thought of his husband being healthy and happy. Tandy thought of the sort of people who do horrible things and try to justify them by saying someone else would've done something far worse. There was nothing worse than what Tandy was thinking. Tandy was the pinnacle of monstrousness, and he knew it full well. He hated to admit it, but part of him reveled in it.

He was content to be a vile thing.

There was a quiet part of Tandy—an indistinct murmur echoing in an empty corner of some unspoiled part of his anatomy—that wished he had developed a more benign fixation. Tandy yearned for an appetite for child pornography, an insatiable craving for videos detailing bestiality.

The day after Victor's surgery, Tandy drove him home from the hospital. During the drive, Tandy's mind raced through all the scenarios, urges, and tendencies he possessed that frightened him. He recalled reading online about a man from Taiwan who became obsessed with ancient Grecian artwork—specifically, limbless figures. Not only would he make his wife position both arms behind her back while he mounted her; he would spray-paint her skin to look like marble. His wife thought it was merely role-playing and was more than happy to oblige. Until one evening when he pushed her arm into the blade of a table saw. As she was bleeding out, he held her in his arms. He wouldn't let go, even when the authorities arrived and struggled to remove him.

There was something beautiful about that story, Tandy felt. He wondered if he was capable of doing something like that to Victor. Of course, that woman had died, and Tandy wanted Victor alive. He wanted his husband to remain sick, but he certainly wanted him to be kept alive.

Tandy glanced at Victor, who was curled in the

passenger seat. In his peripheral vision, he had noticed Victor occasionally appraising him, watching Tandy as he kept both hands on the steering wheel and his eyes trained on the dark road ahead.

"*Breakfast at Tiffany's* tonight?" Victor said, his voice thin and delicate as if an invisible hand had its fingers around his throat.

Tandy smiled at his husband. "I think you'd better rest."

Victor's lips curled downward. Tandy couldn't tell if Victor was upset with his mothering or if something else troubled him.

"What are you thinking about?" Victor asked.

Tandy felt the warmth leave his cheeks. He glanced in the rearview mirror and saw that his face had drained of all color.

He could sense Victor glaring at him—as if he had already worked everything out, been an invisible observer of Tandy's most heinous, horrible thoughts.

Perhaps Tandy should just tell him—just get it over with and let Victor know of his perversions.

"Do you want me to tell you?" Tandy asked, soft and gentle, as though he were approaching a stray dog.

Victor turned away, looking out the side window

and watching the houses as they drifted past.

"I don't want to know," he said flatly.

They never spoke of it again.

As the next few months passed, Tandy derived much secret pleasure from watching Victor change, as if he were transforming into some hideous creature from the kind of black-and-white horror films Tandy used to watch late on Saturday nights. Victor's hair thinned and fell away in clumps, like a sheep being trimmed at the state fair. Victor had been relatively thin when healthy; now his weight began to drop and it wasn't long before Tandy saw the lines of his rib cage pressing against his skin.

Sometimes, when Tandy bumped into Victor in the bathroom, late at night, he wondered if a stranger had crept into the house. One could argue that it's a strain to recognize someone in the dark, but you should, at the very least, always know the person with whom you share a bed. And there were moments when Tandy would turn over, half asleep, see the outline of Victor's face, and wonder what vile thing had crawled into the bed with him. These things never frightened him. In fact, quite the opposite. It inspired a longing—an unquenchable lust—within Tandy.

They made love regularly.

Regularly, that is, when Victor said he felt physically fit enough. There was an undercurrent beneath all their lovemaking sessions—Tandy had a sense that this would soon come to an end, that Victor would be cured forever. It sickened Tandy sometimes, when he thought of what he was actually doing—courting the illness blooming inside his beloved. Tandy knew there would come a time when the illness he had loved in earnest would be a thing of the past, when he and Victor were left to pick up the remnants of what had once been their love. Would they even want to?

There were days when Tandy wondered if Victor still loved him.

"It's going to be bad news," Victor said to Tandy, squeezing his hand a little tighter as they sat in the doctor's office, waiting for the results of a scheduled checkup. "I know it."

"You don't know that, V," Tandy said.

There was a possibility that Victor's cancer could still be active, but Tandy was certain that wasn't so. Victor had obviously been feeling better the last few weeks. Not to mention, how fair would that be for a man as youthful and as full of life as Victor? Naturally, bad news would be music to Tandy's ears, but he knew that wouldn't be fair to his sweet, beloved husband. It wouldn't be fair to keep him like a pet, to be toyed with for his amusement and satisfaction.

After what felt like hours, the doctor arrived and told them the news Tandy had been dreading—Victor was officially cancer-free.

The rest of their conversation dimmed to the hum of white noise. Victor crumpled in his chair like a sheet of rain-soaked parchment. He wept, burying his face in his hands. Tandy wrapped his arm around him, comforting him as best he could, but he felt different somehow, as if Victor were no longer the same person he had once loved. Victor had changed, the way small insects change when they molt and shed their exoskeletons. The cancer—the very thing that had made Victor beautiful to Tandy—was gone and he was left with the remains of Victor's body. Tandy sat there, comforting the strange thing that Victor had become.

Tandy tried for months, but at last, he couldn't bear it any longer. His love for Victor had been removed, the same way a poisonous organ is excised from the human body. When he finally revealed the truth to Victor, Victor broke down again and sobbed. In utter disbelief, Victor begged Tandy to explain himself, but there was very little to say, very little Tandy *could* say to explain why he had fallen out of love with his husband. The sad fact was simple: Tandy had fallen in love with Victor's cancer, and now that the cancer was gone, the love had left too.

"How could you do something like this to me?" Victor asked him, choking on quiet sobs.

"The worst thing I could do would be to pretend I'm not a monster," Tandy said. "But I am a monster. I cannot pretend I'm not."

Victor could hardly speak.

"I think I did once love you," Tandy explained to him. "But I realized I loved your cancer far more than I could have ever loved you."

At dark, I become loathsome.

I think of that story often, especially at nighttime, when I'm feeling particularly prone to insidious and baleful thoughts. I have a link to Tandy's blog saved on my desktop screen. I click on that link every day.

I think of Tandy and what he told Victor: "*I realized I loved your cancer far more than I could have ever loved you.*"

That's how I've come to regard my relationship with life. I'm far more invested in misery, heartache, and despair than in life itself or the actual act of death. There's something decidedly divine about wallowing in the depths of despair, in the throes of melancholy—it's holy, sacred. Death is the final act and cannot be undone. Despair and misery, however, can ferry you to the most consecrated of places within the confines of your mind.

Like Tandy, I'm content to remain a vile, hideous thing, and I curse all those who wish to pluck the black root of cancer from inside me.

At dark, I become loathsome.

CHAPTER ELEVEN

After I return from the funeral home, I heat up one of the frozen entrées I bought at the market early last week. I eat what I can and leave most of the food in the plastic carton I didn't bother to remove to warm up the dinner. I've heard that these frozen dinners are the reason that most people are diagnosed with a specific type of cancer as they reach a certain age. I can't help but wonder if I'll be afforded the same privilege—if I'll be taken from this world the same way my beloved Pema was.

I toss the remnants of my dinner in the garbage bin, swipe the keys from the kitchen counter, and make my way out to the driveway. I climb into the driver's seat, twist the ignition, and am back out on the main road in a matter of seconds. I know exactly where I'm headed: the abandoned one-room schoolhouse on Skiff Mountain.

Part of me expects the client to already be waiting for me when I reach there. He sounded so eager in his correspondence, so excited and impatient to go through the whole ordeal. Little does he know the plans I have for him—the way I plan to permanently absolve him of his agony, his torment, his wretchedness. I wonder: If he knew the ghastly designs I have in mind for him, would he hesitate? Would he restrict his excitement or curtail his enthusiasm?

It's strange, but I look forward to the burial the most now that I've redefined the purpose of the procedure. Sometimes I detested the whole act of digging the hole, lowering the coffin, and burying it with the client inside. Sometimes it seemed such a waste since I was only going to dig them up again and then refill the hole. Now I find myself aching to dig, impatient to stab the ground with my shovel and lift out the earth's secrets until her gaping maw opens before me like the sprawling black mouth of a long-buried behemoth—a creature so abhorrent and detestable that burial seemed too kind a gesture for such an unholy beast.

I notice a small figure beside the dirt road, a hundred or so yards ahead. I squint, my eyes struggling to discern who or what is loitering on the side of the empty roadway. As I ease off the gas and creep closer toward the figure, I realize it's a young boy. No older than eight or nine. He's dressed in a bright orange jacket, a small knitted hat, and dark brown gloves. His hair is perhaps a little longer than it should be for the roundness of his face; however, he carries the extra weight and extra hair length well.

I study the child intently, and for a moment, though he's a stranger to me, I am convinced he is Bailey. I cannot describe it or even explain it, but I am certain that this peculiar boy, who has turned away from the road, is my son. I press on the brakes, almost coming to a stop, wishing I could see the boy's face. He turns back, facing me with a bewildered expression that hardens to anger, an incensed look that seems to say, "I'm not yours. I don't belong to you."

He's right, I think.

I know he's not my son, but part of me wishes he were. I wish it were as easy as driving down an empty country road and coming upon the poor thing on the side of the lane, like a broken bicycle abandoned by its owner.

Yes, an owner, I think to myself.

Bailey belongs to somebody else. He's no longer mine. No longer my sweet child, my innocent boy. He belongs to the world in such a way that only other lost children can understand.

When I realize I'm gawking at the little boy, I set my foot on the accelerator and pull away. I glance in the rearview mirror and see the boy beginning to stroll, likely recognizing the fact that he's out of danger, that the peculiar man with the dozens of metal piercings on his face has abandoned him.

Finally, after another ten minutes or so, I arrive at the small abandoned schoolhouse tucked away at the end of a narrow dirt road. Stretching for a mile or so beyond the rear of the little building is an open field flanked by a row of tall trees that serves as the gateway to a dark forest—the kind of place I expect Bailey was once taken.

I unload the coffin from the rear of the van and haul it toward the center of the field. After I finish digging the hole and lowering the coffin into it, I return to the van and collect the other supplies necessary for the ritual. I make my way to the entrance of the schoolhouse and find the door to be latched and padlocked. Just as I presumed. I grab a pair of bolt cutters from my hardware kit. One snap and the lock clatters to the ground with a loud thud. I kick the chain to the side of the entryway and slowly ease the door open, revealing a small room filled with antique desks and chairs.

I enter, my shoes crunching over dead leaves scattered about the wooden floor. I notice that others have come before me and marked their territory. Graffiti covers the walls of the small schoolhouse—from names of rival gangs in the area to lascivious and detailed illustrations of male and female anatomy. Something in particular catches my eye, and I find myself drawing closer to one wall as if summoned. Letters painted there read *All this happiness makes me sad.*

I think of how true that statement is. Indeed, all this happiness makes me sad. For I will always be sad. I will always be the miserable and wretched thing people are frightened of. I'm a monster, after all.

I begin to unpack my bag, lighting a few candles to brighten the work area. As I pull yet another small candlestick from my satchel, the taper slips from my hands and rolls across the floor toward the open doorway. My gaze follows the candle as it rolls toward Bailey's feet, and I suddenly find my son standing there, gazing at me with a puzzled look.

"What are you doing?" he asks me.

I can hardly find the words. "I'm . . . going to help someone tonight."

"Like that woman you helped last night?" he asks.

I nod gently, fearing that any word might frighten him away, might disturb him and make him never want to return to me.

"You didn't help her," Bailey says. "You killed her."

I feel my throat closing, the words clogging there. "It was . . . what she wanted. I don't expect you to understand, love. It's . . . difficult to describe."

"You hurt her," Bailey says. "You hurt everything."

I creep toward the vision of Bailey, floating in the doorway.

"That's not true, son," I respond. "I do this to help them."

"You don't help people," my son says. "You scare them. Just like you scare me."

Before I can reach out to touch him, Bailey turns and sprints away. I tear after him, dashing down the front steps of the little building, but he's gone. Instead, I see a man standing beside my vehicle—probably no older than thirty or so—with a peculiar look on his face. Arms crossed, he leans on my van for support.

"You're who I'm supposed to meet?" the young man says.

I swallow nervously, eyeing him up and down. "That depends. Are you here for a second chance at life?"

"I'm here because this is easier than permanently ending things," he tells me. "There's something to be said of that."

Of course. He's right, I think to myself. There's

something to be said of those who choose to not permanently end things because of whatever reason. There's a bravery in those who endure hardship, who withstand agony after agony. Little does this young man know that his suffering is almost over, thanks to me, thanks to the vocation I've chosen—the light I've decided to share with the world.

"Shall we begin?" I ask him, motioning him toward the door.

He obeys without much prodding and I think how easy this will be, how delightfully simple.

CHAPTER TWELVE

As soon as the young man crosses the threshold and enters the schoolhouse, he pivots to face me. The first thing I notice about him is his eyes—how they glisten in the candlelight and how they're a green so dark and rich that only jade could compare. He's broad shouldered, lean, and boyishly handsome. As he stands there, looping his index finger and thumb through the belt loop of his jeans and wiping some of his dark hair from the edges of his face, I can't help but admire him.

He's a perfect specimen of masculinity, of brawn, of a tenderness that only few men seem to possess. I assume other men are envious of him—the firmness of his chest, the chiseled structure of his jaw, the plumpness of his lips. *I* am envious of him. I quietly thank

God there are no mirrors in the room, because to compare myself to this young man would be humiliating. It would destroy me entirely. I cringe slightly, sensing myself shrinking, becoming the monster I know myself to be. I wonder what he thinks of me. I wonder what this young man thinks of me as I stand there like a half-wit, my mouth hanging open as if puzzled by the perfection of his body.

I wonder, then, if I'm feeling envy . . . or admiration. After all, I had indulged in an appreciation of the male form many times before I met and married Pema. In fact, I would estimate that my admiration for other men outweighed my fascination with women until I met my late wife. The problem with fooling around with other men is that I've always found it to be so impersonal, so unnecessarily curt—a no-nonsense hand job in the public bathroom stall or anonymous oral sex in the gymnasium showers. Lovemaking, to me, has always been an art form, a consecrated bond—something special and intimate between two people. Looking back from my perspective as a forty-three-year-old widower, I suppose I was a poor lover when I was solely interested in pleasing men; I was looking for something difficult to find among men—companionship, tenderness, and, above all, love.

Still, there's something about this particular young man that excites me, beguiles me, mystifies me. He resembles that charismatic type of charmer that I used to be especially hot for when I was in high school.

I would let him hurt me, I think, pursing my lips and wetting them at the mere thought of the young man's touch.

Then I curse myself for thinking something so vile. Not because I know Pema would disapprove or because I'm a self-loathing bisexual, but because I know if I begin to think of him in such a way, I'll never conjure the nerve to bury him alive. That's what matters most right now: completing the ritual and adding another soul to my list.

I want to paint him.

The thought surprises me.

I haven't felt the urge to paint anything since Pema became ill. And yet, quite suddenly, I'm filled with an intense longing to bask in his presence and immortalize his beauty. I think of how I would capture his essence—the sharpness of his collarbones, the way his cheeks are sculpted, the weariness of his eyes, as if he had seen the world and was bored with what he had witnessed. Obviously, nothing on earth could compare to his beauty. He knows this the same way that all confident and virile men know their worth.

I want to fuck him.

That's the awful, shameful truth. I want nothing more than to bend him over and push myself deep inside him until I'm buried in his guts. But why should I be ashamed of wanting to couple with such an attractive young man? I can't help but wonder if I'm sexually attracted to him or merely jealous of his apparently confident masculinity.

I know for certain that my father would have adored this young man. Even Pema would have wanted to be fucked by him. What woman wouldn't want to be ravished by such a specimen of male beauty? There's something unnerving yet bewitching about him. It excites me.

The young man extends his hand. "I'm Jinx."

Shit, I think. *It's not supposed to happen like this. He's never supposed to tell me his name. Surely, he knows this.*

I silently curse him for his brashness, his unrestrained assertiveness. A naturally suspicious, inherently curious part of me wonders if he told me his name to throw me off my guard, to disarm me. If that was his intention, it's certainly working. Now that I know his name, I can't help but think of him as a person, a fully formed human being—as a lover, a son, a brother. Before he gave me his name, he was none of those things. Now he seems to be a vessel of infinite possibilities.

"You're not supposed to tell me your name," I tell him, pushing past him and returning to my satchel in the candlelit corner of the room. "It doesn't work like that."

Jinx rolls his eyes. "Didn't make much sense to go on without being properly introduced. Even children know to share their name."

"Not with strangers," I say, glancing at him in time to catch his smile.

Jinx replies, perhaps a little too amused, "If you're nice enough, they do."

I ignore his comment. Of course, I'm curious to know what he means, but I dismiss it as inconsequential at the moment. What matters now, most of all, is commencing the ritual and coaxing him into the coffin in the open field behind the schoolhouse. That's where he's destined to end. That's where it is willed for him to find eternal peace.

"We'll begin in here," I tell him, "and start by writing your last will and testament."

Jinx eyes me curiously. "This is legitimate. Right?"

Bewildered by his question, I sense my face scrunching. "Legitimate? I don't know if that's the word I'd use to describe it."

"What word would you use to describe it, then?" he asks, resting both his hands on his hips.

I think for a moment. Finally, the word comes to me:

"It's a purification," I say. "A meeting of the wills, the spirit, the essence of humanity."

Jinx shakes his head. "You don't seem to grasp what I'm asking."

I swallow hard. "Perhaps I don't."

Jinx circles one of the small wooden desks arranged near the entrance of the schoolhouse, sliding his finger across the edge of the seat, wiping away some of the dust there.

"What I mean to say is, this isn't some pathetic excuse to find cock, is it?" he asks, looking pleased and somewhat hopeful.

Blood drains from my cheeks as soon as he utters the word.

"That's what you think this is?"

He hocks up a ball of phlegm and spits it on the floor. "Wouldn't surprise me. I've had men beg me for sex before. I've had grown men crawl at my feet, begging to worship me, pleading to have me use them until I've had enough."

"You think I arranged all this to sleep with you?" I ask.

"Wouldn't surprise me in the least," Jinx says calmly. "In fact, it would make the most sense."

"Would it?" I ask. "Is that what you think?"

"You seemed too eager," he says. "Too eager to meet, too willing to do anything to get a hold of me."

I think of abandoning the ritual altogether. This is the first time I've been accused of something so heinous.

"Perhaps you're not as serious about changing your life as I thought you were," I say, trying to sound dismissive.

"Oh, I am," he says. "I want nothing more than to be *purified*—to be born again, to be resurrected and shown how wondrous life can be. But I need to know you're the right person to guide me on this journey."

I sense my eyebrows furrow. "Well, this is the first time a client has ever asked me to prove myself."

"That's because most people are blind idiots," Jinx says. "They go wherever you tell them to go, like sheep."

It's true. I realize that during the few months I've

been performing these rituals, most of my clients have done little to question me. They've nearly all obeyed my commands with no more than the slightest of hesitations. Of course, there's the signed contract that nullifies their requests; however, it's alarming to recognize just how malleable most people are, how they feel they deserve whatever suffering you plan on inflicting on them.

"What can I do to prove to you that I'm in this for your best interest?" I ask, hoping I can find a way to relax him so that I can dispatch him as efficiently and easily as possible.

Jinx thinks, visibly searching his mind for an answer. Finally, an idea seems to come to him. He reaches into a pocket and pulls out a small sack of green marbles, which he pours into the palm of his hand.

"Swallow this," he says, plucking one from the collection and holding it out to me.

I shake my head, wondering if I've heard him correctly.

"You want me to swallow a marble?"

Before I can say another word, he dumps all the marbles back into the sack and cinches it closed.

"I knew you couldn't be trusted," he says.

"Why?" I ask. "Why a marble?"

Jinx smiles, pleased with my question. He loosens the black string on the bag and pulls out a marble about the size of a quail egg.

"My grandfather gave me these when I was very little," Jinx explains. "I've kept them in a box underneath my bed. They mean a lot to me because they meant a lot to him, but they're probably worthless otherwise. Probably bought them at some market in Hanoi when he was stationed overseas during the war."

"So, why do you want me to swallow one whole if they mean so much to you?" I ask him.

"Because they mean a lot to me," he says. "If this means a lot to you, you'll do something that means a lot to me. I can't think of anything more fitting."

I stare at the little marble resting on his palm. It seems to whisper to me: *Come to me, follow me . . .*

Without another moment of hesitation, I swipe the marble from Jinx's hand and push it into my mouth. It feels unnatural, sitting on the shelf of my tongue. Before I can consider an alternative, I gulp and send the marble plummeting down my throat. My esophagus burns a little, stretched as if a hand has reached down my throat and rearranged my stomach.

Jinx eyes me, clearly still somewhat uncertain.

"Open your mouth," he demands.

I obey, opening my mouth and allowing him to shine his phone's flashlight between my gums.

Once he's satisfied, he pulls his phone away and smiles.

"You lost your marble though," I tell him.

"You'll shit it out eventually," Jinx says with another smile.

"Did I pass?"

Jinx's face softens a little. He reaches into a different pocket and pulls out a small sheet of paper.

"Something for your troubles," he tells me as he hands me the paper.

It's covered with a mess of chicken scratch—a bacchanal of shapes and figures assembled in disorienting unison, a screeching symphony of different silhouettes rendered by an amateur surrealist.

"You draw?" I ask.

"I didn't create this," he says. "Somebody else did."

"Who?" I ask.

Jinx simpers coyly. "Better not tell you yet."

My eyes return to the jumbled mess, the cacophony of confusion on the paper. "What do you call it?"

"*An Anatomically Incorrect Angel*," he says, grinning from ear to ear.

As he laughs, I study the illustration further and begin to think I perhaps finally see the artist's intention. Yes, it resembles something like an anatomically incorrect celestial being—something we will never know and never understand. Perhaps that's for the best. Perhaps we're not meant to.

CHAPTER THIRTEEN

I set the illustration of the "anatomically incorrect angel" aside and rummage through my rucksack until I find the paperwork Jinx is supposed to sign. I unfold the documents and grab a pen from my bag. Out of the corner of my eye, I notice Jinx observing me with keen attentiveness.

"Before we begin, I need your signature on a few forms," I explain, brandishing the papers. "You can feel free to read them over or just sign."

"Surely, you don't expect me to sign without reading what I'm getting myself into, do you?" he asks me.

"Some people just want to get it over with," I tell him, handing him the sheets.

"I don't intend to just 'get this over with,'" he says. "I intend to make this last. I want this to be an experience."

I wince a little. It's the first time I've ever heard a client so enthusiastic, so keen to undergo the ritual.

I watch Jinx as he studies the documents. I bite my lower lip—a nervous habit—when I see him shake his head and mutter beneath his breath. Finally, he looks at me, frowning.

"You accept no responsibility if something should go wrong?" he asks. "You can't expect people to sign this garbage."

I'm unsure how to respond. Jinx doesn't seem agitated, just grim and humorless, as if he were a mourner grieving the loss of a recently departed loved one.

"I thought you were serious about this," I say. "I understand if it's too much for you."

"Too much for me?"

"Some people can't handle it," I say. "They're too . . . scared."

"It's not a matter of fear," he responds.

"Then perhaps you don't need my services after all," I say to him. "It's always a relief when clients are honest about their misgivings from the get-go."

"I have no misgivings."

I eye him up and down, then gesture to the contract once more. "Then you'll sign?"

Jinx hesitates slightly, disarmed by my challenge to

him. He takes the pen and scrawls his name across the dotted line on the very last page of the document. Before he can say anything else, I grab the papers and shove them back into my rucksack.

"It's for the best," I say. "You won't be disappointed."

"Certainly not for this kind of money," Jinx says.

Yes, the matter of the money. In my mind, I thank him for reminding me. Of course, we could settle the arrangement now. But I'll have his clothing soon enough and I can always take the funds from his wallet, like I did with the old woman after I buried her.

I kneel on the floor, fishing inside the rucksack again. This time I pull out a blank sheet of lined paper, which I set on the small desk that separates us.

"An art lesson?" he says.

"A last will and testament," I explain. "It can be written however you please. A list of personal items you'd like to relinquish. A letter you'd like to write to someone."

"A letter?"

"Yes. Maybe somebody you've hurt? Somebody whose kindness you've yet to repay?"

I watch Jinx as he ponders, visibly searching his mind for a response.

"Can't think of anybody who has earned an apology from me," he says, crossing his arms across his chest. "But there's someone—something—I think about every day. It gnaws at my mind. Keeps me awake at night."

"Yes?"

"It's about a dog," Jinx tells me. "A fucking dog. Can you believe how asinine that sounds?"

"Some people love dogs," I remind him.

"I think that's why I think about it so often," he says. "Because I loved that dog with all my heart."

Jinx's eyes flash to me for a response, but I say nothing. I don't really understand—I've never had a pet—and perhaps he can see that on my face.

"Before my dad left me and my mom, he found a dog. Kept it tied with wire to a wooden post outside, behind our shed," Jinx explains. "My dad loved that fucking dog. I loved it too. Big floppy ears. Cold, wet snout always pressing on you, felt like an ice cube on your leg. Taught him tricks. Roll over. Play dead. Shit like that. Fed him what we didn't eat. Wasn't much. But sometimes my dad wouldn't eat on purpose. Just so the dog could. Slept at his feet every night."

The color of Jinx's eyes begins to dim, and it isn't long before they're two reflecting pools as murky as ocean water; I could easily drown in them if I stared long enough.

"But we started running out of food, and soon

the dog went a week without eating," Jinx says. "When one thing changes, everything else does too. Its eyes became sunken pits. Its ribs pressed against its skin. And one day, when my dad went to untie it from the post, the dog leaped at him and bit through his hand."

Jinx looks at me, as if expecting me to react or to say something to comfort him.

I don't.

"So, he took a shovel and flattened the dog's head with it," Jinx says. "It yelped and wobbled back on its hind legs. I watched its smashed, wet head shaking back and forth. Its tail went between its legs and it pissed itself. My dad slammed the shovel against the dog's back legs. It fell over, whimpering. It dragged itself away from the post and back behind some rocks. It crawled out there to die. But before it died, I remember how it looked at my dad, all confused and hurt. Dying in the middle of a question."

Silence leaches into the small schoolhouse for what feels like hours, though I know it's merely moments. I search my mind for something to say, but I cannot conjure anything that would comfort or even make the faintest bit of sense.

"I think if I was going to write something," Jinx says,

"I'd write a letter to that dog. I'd ask him what that question was. Hopefully, I'd have an answer for him."

I smile awkwardly, not sure what to say or do next. I think Jinx can tell that I'm uncertain how best to proceed.

"Is there someone *you'd* write a letter to?" he asks.

I sense my face paling at the question. This is the first time a client has ever questioned me, probed me for more information.

I think for a moment—wondering what I should say, wondering if I should lie or simply tell the truth. After all, there is someone I would like to write a letter to—someone I think about almost every day.

"Yes," I say to him. "I'd write a letter to the man I almost cheated on my wife with."

Jinx tilts his head, quizzically studying my face.

"It was when I was taking my wife to the hospital regularly for her chemotherapy," I explain. "I excused myself from the room and wandered down the hallway to the men's restroom. I approached a urinal and unzipped, pulling myself completely out and just standing there for a moment. I was afraid of what was to come."

"What was to come?"

"Her dying," I say. "So, I wondered if I should. It wouldn't be the first time I had pleasured myself in a public place. I felt so cornered. I felt surrounded by death and pain. I wanted to feel something—anything but the unbearable agony . . . When I was a teenager, a dear friend of mine was killed, along with his parents, in a car crash. In a way, he was more than a friend. I had loved him, though in my darkest moments of reflection, I knew he would never love me. But I remained hopeful until he was finally taken from this world. I, like many of my peers, attended his funeral, looking somber and wearing expensive black.

"Not long after the funeral, a dull gathering was held at the church recreation hall—children were prohibited from running or playing and were to remain chaperoned by their parents at all times. Somehow, I sneaked away and crept down to the basement of the recreation center where there was a small bathroom. I made my way over to the urinal and began masturbating. I'll never forget the shame I felt—the disgust I carried with me—for pleasuring myself while others mourned and sobbed at the loss of innocent life.

"As I thought of that moment, while I stood with my pants around my ankles in the hospital restroom, I wondered if I had always been attracted to other people's suffering. Perhaps it had been impressed upon me, indelibly smeared upon my mind like an invisible ink stain, at some young age, when I knew no better. Something shrieked at me, in my quietest moment of reflection, and told me I had always been this way. I had always been a monster.

"I stroked myself, fighting off thoughts of Pema suffering as best I could, until the bathroom door swung open and someone marched in. I immediately hoisted my pants up around my waist, pocketing myself in my underwear as I began to go soft. I turned slightly and glimpsed a young man making his way toward the bathroom's only private stall. His hair was buzzed short, like a sailor. He had nearly a perfect figure—broad shoulders tapering to a thin waist. A former athlete, you could be certain.

"As he passed me, our eyes met. I'm not quite sure what possessed me to even look at him in the first place since I had always been uncomfortable interacting with other men in public restrooms, but there was something so alluring about him. His gaze lingered on me and I sensed myself stiffening once more.

"He glanced down at my crotch, then back up to meet my gaze. His lips creased with a polite-looking smile before his face hardened with a look that seemed to say, 'Follow me.' He inched closer to the bathroom stall, eyeing me with his wordless invitation. I thought for a moment, freezing as I stood there. Did I dare follow him? What wonders awaited me if I did?

"In the next instant, I zipped my pants and dashed out of the restroom. I wasn't certain if his eyes were still glued on me when I left, but I didn't care. There were many things I would do to Pema. Many unspeakable things that might make some think of me as a monster. But I knew full well how much I loved and cared for my wife, even though she was so ill. I would be damned before I betrayed her by seeking out companionship with another man."

I stare at Jinx for a beat too long and he seems to notice. I wonder if I was right to tell him something so personal, so excruciatingly private.

"You never saw him again?" he asks me.

"No," I reply.

I'm surprised at myself for revealing such an intimate moment—a moment I had no plans to share with another person as long as I lived. I wonder why I decided to tell the story of the man at the urinal in the public bathroom, why I let my guard down and allowed Jinx the privilege of reveling in such a private, revealing moment. Is it because on some primitive level I fancy him? Is it because it's nighttime, seeing as I become quite loathsome at dark? It's the rancid type of behavior

I expect from a love-starved lothario, not a grieving widower.

"I never told my wife about that," I say, glancing away out of embarrassment.

"I'm sure she knows," he says. "She had to have known she married a queer man."

"She knew what I was," I agree. "She knew from the day she met me until she died."

Jinx's smile begins to dissipate as if the very presence of death had intruded upon our meeting.

"She died—?" he asks.

"A few years ago," I tell him, my eyes lowering.

"I'm sorry."

"My son and I were too," I say.

"You have a son—?" he asks, leaning forward.

I curse myself for saying something so idiotic. Should I tell him about Bailey? Does he even deserve to know about my precious boy? Even if he apologizes for my loss, wistfully condemns such a heinous act, it won't matter much. His remorsefulness won't bring Bailey back.

"I did have a son," I tell him.

The words feel unnatural—why did I speak about Bailey in past tense? There's a chance he's still out there, after all. There's a possibility—however remote, however faint—that he's still out there, waiting to be found.

"I *do* have a son, I should say," I correct myself. "He was taken from me. The police have been looking for him, but they don't seem that hopeful anymore."

"They always prefer to be grim about things, don't they?" Jinx says. "What was his name?"

I pause for an instant, wondering if I should tell him. I'm surprised we've spent this much time talking. Usually, I prefer my clients to be as unresponsive as possible, but for some inexplicable reason, I enjoy talking to Jinx.

"His name was Bailey," I say.

"They think they know what happened to him?" Jinx asks.

It's a terrible question, a horrible reminder that there's a convincing likelihood that Bailey suffered at the hands of his captor.

"They have their theories," I say.

"But you don't believe them?" he asks.

"There's a part of me that hopes he's still out there. Waiting to be found."

I reach into my pocket and pull out my wallet. I slide out a small Polaroid picture of Bailey I took one summer afternoon, when he had decided to dress up in Pema's wedding gown. I gaze at the photograph for a few moments, studying the intricate bouquet of lilies in the boy's hands and admiring the way Pema had pinned back some of his hair with a barrette in the shape of a butterfly.

I pass the photograph to Jinx and watch him as his eyes go over the small picture.

"Liked to dress up?" he asks.

"All the time," I reply. "His mother always encouraged his imagination."

Jinx glares at me. "But you hated it."

I'm surprised at his brashness. But perhaps I shouldn't be. I let down my guard, softening slightly.

"I didn't want him to get hurt," I say. "The world is cruel to people who are different."

"You knew he was gay," Jinx says.

I sense myself pale at the word. I *did* think that but tried not to associate the word with my suspicions. After all, Bailey was a child. It didn't seem fair to assign him a role so early in his life. Still, there were fears I always possessed for my little boy.

"I wanted him to be happy," I tell Jinx. "But I was scared for him."

"Because you knew."

I sense tears beading in the corners of my eyes.

"Because I knew he was a faggot," I say, trembling a little. "I called him that one day. I didn't mean for him to hear me, but he did. I didn't want him to be like me—a self-loathing queer man."

Jinx lowers his gaze for a moment, then stares firmly at me.

"Children lose their innocence when they realize that adults can hurt them," he says.

I shake my head in a futile attempt to hurl the unpleasant thoughts from my mind. "I never wanted to hurt him. I just didn't want him to be like me. I spent so many years hating myself, loathing who I was, until I met Pema. If he's still alive—still out there somewhere—I hope he doesn't remember the word I called him that day. Maybe that's why he hasn't come home. Because he thinks that's all I think of him."

I stand unmoving for a moment, my limbs hard and stiff as if they were made from beeswax. A curtain of silence hangs over both me and Jinx, the little one-room schoolhouse feeling like a vacuum of all sound.

I realize I shouldn't have told Jinx any of that. It was a mistake. I'm not here to soften my temperament. I'm here to set him free from his suffering. I'm here to end his agony.

"I shouldn't have told you that," I say to Jinx, wiping some of the moisture from my eyes.

"Why not?" he asks. "It's the truth, isn't it?"

"We're not here for me," I say. "We're here for you. Your pain. Your suffering."

Jinx seems to immediately understand me.

"You need to undress," I tell him.

"What about my last will and testament?" he asks.

I merely shake my head, gesturing to his shirt and pants.

Jinx obeys without further direction, unbuttoning his shirt and sliding it off to reveal a physique that a Grecian athlete might be envious of. The perfect lines of his abdominals glisten in the candlelight, and for a moment, I stare at him unreservedly. Then Jinx glances at me and I immediately pull my gaze away.

Jinx turns to face the wall, unbuckles his belt, and starts to unbutton his jeans. He lowers his pants until they're crumpled around his ankles. He steps out of the jeans, then flings them onto a nearby desk. In my peripheral vision, I notice the firmness and plumpness of his hairless buttocks. I don't dare look directly for fear he'll once again think I am up to something. If only he knew the truth. If only he knew my real plans for him.

Finally, he pivots slightly to face me. When he does, I can't stop myself; my gaze is immediately drawn to his freshly shaved manhood. His cock—limp and roughly average in size—dangles obscenely. I can't help but admire him as he rubs his testicles with one hand.

"Well—?" he says, eyeing me, begging me to look at him in all his naked glory.

I find myself unable to speak at first, far too enraptured with the sight of him—his fully exposed manhood, his nearly perfect body.

"Please sit," I say at last, gesturing to one of the chairs.

He obeys, sitting down and covering his crotch with both hands as if suddenly bashful, suddenly aware that I'm delighting in his nakedness.

I pull the plastic bag containing a damp washcloth from my rucksack and approach him gently.

"It might be a little cold," I warn him as I open the bag.

When I press the cloth against his shoulders, he winces slightly.

"Sorry," I say, although I'm not.

I'm secretly loving every moment that passes between us, devoted to him in a way he'll never know. For a moment, I wonder if I really want to bury him alive. It would be an insult to his beauty, after all.

Gliding the wet cloth along his collarbone, I then move farther down his body until I reach his pectorals and finally his sculpted abdominals. As I scrub his chest with tender force, he shifts the position of his hands, covering his private area. I glance down at his groin and notice that his cock has grown considerably. Jinx slides a hand over his dick, protecting it from my sight.

I hesitate, but I know it must be done. Before Jinx can say anything, I let the washcloth wander below his waist until it arrives at his manhood. He moves his hand out of the way and I see that his cock is fully erect, sprouting from between his legs in a clear invitation. I wash him there, maneuvering around his dick. The whole time, Jinx's gaze remains fixed on me, as if he were begging me to proceed, to cross the threshold and take him as he wants to be taken.

I see the expression on his face shift, but before he can open his mouth and say anything, I pull the washcloth away and toss it aside. I grab the white linen robe I left nearby and pass it to him.

"Get dressed in this," I tell him. "I'll wait."

Jinx takes the robe and scurries off into the corner, where he begins to dress. As he turns from me, I wonder if his silent request for more than a thorough washing was an attempt to conquer me and regain control of the situation. I wonder if he somehow has discerned my ghastly plans for him.

For a moment, I pity him—his bodily perfection,

his grace. Perhaps, in another life, the two of us might have found comfort in one another. Perhaps we would have fallen in love and lived joyously, without pain or agony, without suffering, the way other men from other eras found love and protected their romances from the blight of the world.

That's not possible now.

The two of us are inexorably fixed in our roles: he, the prisoner; I, his captor.

When he finishes dressing, Jinx returns to me like a lovelorn specter.

"Be careful," I say. "We're headed somewhere dark."

CHAPTER FOURTEEN

After a short walk, we arrive at the burial site, where the coffin that will be Jinx's final resting place is waiting in a shallow hole.

For some inexplicable reason, I find myself unsettled, distressed, as if I could feel the green marble Jinx forced me to swallow sinking, like a concrete block, in my stomach.

I can tell there's something Jinx wants to say, something he yearns to tell me. Whatever it is can wait, however, and must wait. This is the moment I've been thinking of since we first met—his burial.

"Can you manage to get in?" I ask him, gesturing to the coffin.

On hands and knees, Jinx crawls into the coffin and arranges himself like an embalmed corpse. I quietly delight in the fact that this will be easier than I anticipated. Given Jinx's impertinence, I expected some resistance from him. I expected him to hesitate or even completely refuse to climb inside the coffin. It surprises me to find him so amenable, so suddenly courteous and cooperative.

I study his face in the glow of candlelight and wonder what he's thinking. I wonder what his last thoughts will be once I close the coffin lid and he's a forgotten secret that belongs to the darkest recesses of my memory.

"You might feel unwell during the first couple of minutes," I explain. "But that will soon pass. I'll start the stopwatch and won't come back for you until the thirty minutes are up. Does that make sense?"

Jinx nods gently.

It's peculiar to find him so suddenly quiet. Perhaps he is reflecting, wondering why he agreed to this in the first place. This is what he wanted though. I'm only too glad to offer him the same peace, the same compassion and spiritual freedom, that I so desperately yearn for.

As I begin to close the coffin lid, Jinx grabs my hand. For a moment, he says nothing. His face bears a lost and bewildered expression.

"There's a reason I came to you tonight," he says.

His reason doesn't matter, but I can't stop myself from saying, "Yes—?"

"I knew your son," Jinx says with a sudden smirk.

I lean closer, thinking I've misheard him somehow. "You . . . *knew* . . . Bailey?"

Jinx's mouth tightens for a moment before he finally pushes the words out: "I'm the one who took him from you."

I can scarcely believe what he's said. I shake my head, not wanting to accept his words, wanting to have misheard him, misunderstood him.

Before I can respond, Jinx grabs the coffin lid and slams it shut. I think of opening the coffin and begging him to repeat what he said. But some inexplicable force commands me to seize my shovel, tighten my grip on its handle, and begin to cover the coffin with dirt. Against my better judgment, almost before I'm aware that I've begun the task, I do just that. Soon the coffin's lid completely disappears.

I've no sense of time passing, but at last I look down and realize that the grave is filled. I let the shovel slip from my hands and it clatters on the ground. I'm without movement for a moment. I'm finished. I've done what I had promised myself I would do—I buried him and set him free.

But the thing he told me right before the coffin lid closed rolls around in my mind like a piece of rotten fruit circling a small drain.

I repeat the sentence again and again inside my mind: *I'm the one who took him from you. I'm the one who took him from you. I'm the one who took him from you.*

What could he have meant? What did he mean? Was he confessing? If so, why?

Even worse, if not, why would he joke about something so abhorrent?

I pace the ground near the grave. Perhaps it was a prank—something he said to amuse himself.

But what if he was telling me the truth? What if he had done something to Bailey? What if he knows the exact whereabouts of my son? If I leave him buried there as I intended, I will never know.

I struggle to decide what to do. I swore to end his misery, but now? Do I leave him there? Or dig him out and question him? I'll never get him back in the coffin again if I unbury him. That much is certain.

If he knows what happened to my son, that's all that truly matters to me. That's all I've cared about since the day Bailey vanished.

I could leave him there to rot—until his body became a carpet of sweets for ants, maggots, and other insects to feast upon—or I could deliver him from his prison.

Unsure, I stand still, listening to the faint murmur of wind rustling through the nearby trees as if it were a voice ordering me to dig until I find him again. The wind's calling settles my mind. Yes, that's what I need to do: unbury Jinx and make him confess everything he knows about my precious Bailey.

My pacing has taken me away from the shovel, which I'd dropped in some weeds. I practically jump over to it, grab it, and begin to dig. The ground seems to yawn open at me, inviting me deeper and deeper until I come upon the coffin lid once more. I scramble to my hands and knees and clear the dirt and gravel from the lid until it's completely uncovered. I climb out of the hole and strain to open the coffin. It seems to take forever before the lid comes free. Lying there, exactly where I left him, is Jinx. His eyelids flutter open and he finds me immediately. For a moment, he doesn't speak, merely looks at me with a blank expression. Did he somehow know I might not come back for him? Is he silently cursing me for my cruelty?

"That didn't feel like thirty minutes," he says.

I stammer at first, unsure what to say. "It's—it's getting late. I want to be sure we have enough time for everything . . . Are you okay?"

Jinx nods. He climbs out of the coffin, then crawls on the ground like a toddler.

"Careful," I tell him. "Don't rush too much."

He sits beside the grave, hugging his knees against his chest and breathing in short, shallow gasps. Before I say another word, he leans back in the tall grass and stares heavenward. I watch him for a moment, wondering what he's thinking, wondering if it's both too soon and too late to ask about my son.

I'm still trying to decide, when Jinx's gaze snaps to me.

"There's more to be done?" he asks.

This isn't the right time or the right place. I've waited years for this answer. I can certainly wait a few more moments. I need Jinx to continue trusting me.

"Yes," I tell him. "Follow me."

I drag the shovel behind me as we walk, slowly, with uncertain steps, through the tall grass toward the one-room schoolhouse. I don't bother to turn and see if Jinx is following me or not. I know he is. As we move, a blast of cold air surrounds me; it seems to push me along the path as if I were headed toward something from which I can never turn back, something for which I've waited years: *an answer.*

CHAPTER FIFTEEN

We finally reach the schoolhouse at the edge of the small field. Jinx shuffles along as if he were dazed, as if he were a convicted felon being led toward a crowd chanting for his public execution.

I wonder if I should have killed him, if I should have left him there in the coffin to die slowly. After all, if he actually was responsible for Bailey's disappearance, a live burial would be only too good for him. But I need to know. I need to know what became of my son.

Jinx halts at the small building's threshold, seemingly hesitant to enter. I give him a gentle push, the way a shepherd might steer a stray member of his flock, and Jinx obeys without objection. It's as if that's all he needed—a gentle push, a tender reminder to move forward and not back. Perhaps that's what we all need. Perhaps that's all it will take to coax the information from him, to learn what happened to my son.

I notice Jinx is shivering a little, trembling as he folds his arms and braces himself against one of the room's exposed wooden beams.

"Sit there," I say, gesturing to a chair near one of the small desks.

Jinx does without comment.

For a moment, I'm uncertain what's to be done, how to best approach him. After all, this was never the plan. I had absolutely no intention of ever seeing Jinx again after I buried him. I had every intention of leaving him there to rot, to finally be freed of the suffering that he implied nearly paralyzes him. But now, I'm not convinced that he deserves unrestricted access to paradise. Perhaps the better thing to do would be to see to it that he cannot hurt anybody else as long as he's alive. And if he's guilty, I know what I want for him—for him to suffer.

"How do you feel?" I ask, turning away to rummage through my rucksack. "A bit lightheaded maybe?"

"Yeah," he says. "I feel like I might split apart like wet paper."

"Good," I say. "That means it's working."

"You make it sound like a drug," he says.

I laugh a little. "Maybe it is."

I locate the item I'm searching for in my bag: a small hammer with a red handle. For some reason, I tossed it into the rucksack when I was packing for tonight. I don't know why, but it seemed like a good idea to bring it along. I quietly thank God for thinking ahead.

"You said something before I buried you," I say.

Jinx looks at me queerly. "Did I—?"

I send him a look of disgust, begging him to cut the pretense. "You know you did."

Jinx's face hardens—now that he's caught, he knows there's no way to deny it any longer.

"Yes, I did," he says quietly.

I approach him, tightening my fist around the hammer's handle.

"What did you mean when you said you took him from me?" I ask.

Jinx glances at the hammer and a smile creases his face. "Are you planning on making good use of that?"

"Depends," I tell him. "Don't lie to me."

"I wasn't lying to you," he says. "There's a reason I said what I said."

I sense my cheeks beginning to heat red. My free hand clenches into a fist.

"What did you do to him?" I ask, my voice dimming to a mere whisper.

"You're not going to hurt me, are you?" Jinx asks.

There's a strangeness in the way he asks, almost as if he regretted that I hadn't harmed him yet, almost as if he were looking forward to the agony, the pain I could invite upon him.

"They'll be picking clumps of your hair from the end of this hammer if you lie to me," I warn him.

Jinx's voice trembles a little as he says, "I'd like to see you try that."

I lean over him until I can smell him, until the scent of his grave fills my nostrils.

"What do you know about my son?"

Jinx crosses his legs, simpering, pleased I finally asked.

"I know everything there is to know about your precious Bailey," he says. "A charming little boy. So filled with life."

I loathe the sound of my son's name in Jinx's mouth. He pronounces it as if it were something indecent, something decidedly vile.

"Do you know what he told me?" Jinx asks, looking out one of the nearby windows. "He said he wondered why God had made him a boy when he wanted so desperately to be a girl. Did he ever tell you that?"

I have both hands on the hammer's handle now,

twisting it in my hands. I am sorely tempted to strike him with it, to conjure a nightmare upon him.

Wetness gathers in the corners of my eyes at the reminder that Bailey never told me much of anything. Before Pema died, he always went to his mother for more urgent, more personal matters. He didn't trust me, as if he knew I would condemn him or hate him. After Pema's death, I realize, Bailey was left alone with his fears and feelings.

"He never told me that," I tell Jinx gently.

"It was amusing to listen to an eight-year-old's assessment of gender," Jinx says. "He told me that he thought his spirit went into the wrong body when he was born. That's amusing, isn't it? Does the soul even have a gender?"

Jinx looks at me, visibly expecting me to answer. But I don't.

"Well—?" he prods me.

"I don't know," I reply. "I haven't given it much thought."

I slightly relax my grip on the hammer, trying to stay calm, to learn Jinx's secrets.

"What did you do to him?" I ask Jinx, sitting across from him in one of the small school chairs. "Is he alive somewhere?"

"What makes you think that?" Jinx asks.

I slam the hammer on the desk and the wood splits apart like wet paper.

"Don't fuck with me about this," I say, not quite shouting. "You can't confess like that and then expect to play coy. I want you to tell me everything you know."

Jinx looks away for a moment, closing his eyes.

"If I tell you, I want you to promise me something," he says, his green eyes staring steadily into mine. My piercings have no effect on him.

"I'm not promising anything."

"Then you won't get what you're after," Jinx tells me.

I straighten, brandishing the hammer in front of him.

"After a while, you'll tell me anything I want to know," I retort. "I'm not worried."

Jinx glares at me challengingly, but I don't back down. I rise from my chair and tower over him, tossing the hammer from hand to hand.

"What's it going to be?" I ask.

Jinx falters for an instant. Then he clears the catch in his throat and begins to speak, slowly.

"Bailey was a mere boy when he came to me that day I met him on Church Street," Jinx says. "But he left this world something else. Something truly marvelous . . .

Pain and suffering can change a person. It can transform them into something miraculous . . ."

In the next instant, I lunge at Jinx, knocking over the desk separating us.

"What did you do to him?" I ask him once we're face-to-face.

Jinx doesn't answer—just stares at me with a soundless message that seems to say that he will only tell me if I do exactly what he says.

"He's dead, isn't he?" I ask.

Jinx hesitates, visibly reluctant to say anything.

"Yes," he says at last. "I killed him. Burned the body until there was nothing but bones left. Then I burned the ashes too."

I close my eyes, willing it to somehow be undone. But it's no use.

I slam the hammer against the side of Jinx's face. Stunned, the younger man wobbles there for an instant before he slumps out of the chair and lands on the floor with a sickening thud.

I brace him, pinning him to the ground, ready to bring the hammer down for a second time.

"How could you?" I ask. "Why did you do this?"

Jinx, drifting in and out of consciousness, trembles and writhes.

"Tell me," I beg him. "Tell me why."

Jinx's eyelids flutter open; a dark line of blood creeps along his brow.

"Where's the drawing?" Jinx asks.

"What?"

"The drawing I gave you," he says. "It was one of the last things Bailey drew for me."

I grab the sheet of paper and regard the drawing once more. Now that I know, everything about the illustration reminds me of Bailey and how he used to draw—the confident lines, the overambitious loops, all signs that tell me this once belonged to him.

"Why did you seek me out?" I ask Jinx.

Jinx smiles. "I thought it would be special to spend Bailey's birthday together. He would've been ten years old today. Unless I'm mistaken?"

Of course, Jinx is not mistaken. It's true that Bailey would have been ten years old today. My precious Bailey would be alive and here today if it weren't for Jinx.

"I think about your son often," Jinx continues. "How he smelled. How he felt. How he didn't cry, even when I had asked him to undress in that tiny, windowless room where he died."

I shudder slightly, Jinx's words filling me like black tar.

"What did you do to him?" I ask, quietly dreading

the answer. I shove the last picture Bailey ever drew into my pocket—anything to keep my sweet boy close to me.

Jinx exhales, smiling. "You're sure you want to know each and every detail?"

I nod, squeezing my eyelids shut. "I need to know."

"I've wanted to tell you about this for so long," Jinx says, his face and voice thawing with warmth as he looks at me. "When I told you that story in the chat room, I was surprised that you never told me to stop. Not once. I think you enjoyed it. I'd hoped you would . . . Did you touch yourself after?"

Did he really just ask me that?

I want to lie. I want to tell him off, tell him how disgusting that story was. But I can't. I can't bear to lie to him, though I know full well he'd lie to me without a second thought.

I nod. "Yes. I touched myself . . . I—liked it . . ."

Jinx's eyes widen with visible excitement and anticipation.

"Let me tell you what I did to your son," Jinx says eagerly. "It's okay if you like it . . ."

But I don't think I can take it much longer. Part of me was once curious about all the things Bailey had endured before he left this world. That bit of curiosity is now permanently erased. I don't need to know. I never truly needed to know.

"I don't think I can bear it," I tell Jinx, choking on my own saliva and snot.

Jinx looks disappointed only for a moment. "You don't want to hear about all the little cruelties he endured before I finally killed him?"

His words are sharp enough to disembowel me, to ravage me like woodland predators feasting on a lifeless corpse, to pierce me with cruel, unforgiveable torture. I feel like I might come apart—my very bones will disconnect from one another, and I'll be reduced to a steaming pile of human viscera.

Bile rises in my throat. I feel like I'll vomit. Part of me hopes I will—anything to purge myself of the agony, the unbearable knowledge that poor Bailey had been defiled by Jinx before he perished. The awful thought is enough to push me across the invisible barrier separating us, to make me take the hammer and bash it against Jinx's head, to destroy him just as he destroyed my beloved son.

Before I realize it, I'm on hands and knees with vomit pouring from my open mouth as though a rusted tap had been unscrewed deep inside me. I strain, gagging as I release more fluid to spread across the floorboards.

When I'm finished vomiting, I can hardly breathe. My vision is blurred by my tears.

I straighten and do my best to catch my breath. Jinx says nothing, simply watches as I struggle to swallow and wipe my eyes.

It's then I make the final decision—the decision I have been putting off since he first made his horrible confession. I'm going to kill Jinx. I'm going to crack his skull open with the hammer and bury him in the grave he's already, all too briefly, occupied.

I raise the hammer. As I'm about to bring it down onto him, there's a flicker of movement in my peripheral vision—a small, dark shape stirring at the entrance of the room. I look away from Jinx and see a child's silhouette standing in the open doorframe. It's Bailey's apparition.

He seems reluctant to enter, his somber face barely lit by the surrounding candlelight.

I warily approach my son as he stands at the room's threshold.

"What are you doing here?" I ask him.

Bailey doesn't say anything. His head moves and I realize his gaze is tracking along my arm, all the way to the blood-soaked end of the hammer I'm holding.

I swallow hard, recognizing the sight I must be—the monster I must resemble.

I wince slightly, almost wishing I could somehow pull myself out of my own skin suit and fly away until I'm cosmic dust.

"Do I scare you?" I ask him.

Bailey nods gently, cowering.

My muscles loosen and I feel the jewelry attached to my face begin to sag.

"I don't mean to scare you," I say. "But you shouldn't be here."

Bailey studies Jinx lying on the floor, obviously noticing the blood pooling beneath his head.

"He's all right," I say. "I promise."

I motion for my son to follow me out the door of the one-room schoolhouse, onto the small building's front steps.

"Will you do me a favor?" I ask. "Will you promise you'll leave this place? You shouldn't be here."

Bailey bows his head, knowing full well I'm right.

Recognizing his glumness and thinking quickly, I pull his illustration of the angel from my pocket, unfold the paper, and show it to my little boy.

"Do you know what this is?" I ask.

Bailey nods.

"Keep this with you and she'll always protect you," I say, passing him the sheet of paper.

He grasps it tightly, staring at the image.

"Go home," I tell him. "You shouldn't be out this late."

I pat Bailey on the head and send him on his way, watching his little spirit weave between our parked vehicles and meander away until the moonlight can follow him no longer.

When Bailey is gone, I return to the schoolroom. Jinx has rolled onto his side, doubling over in visible agony.

I don't say anything. After all, what is there left to say?

After what feels like hours, Jinx speaks:

"Kill me," he says, his breathing ragged and shallow. "Just fucking do it."

I neither speak nor move. Since I saw Bailey, my resolve has disappeared. After all, it's one thing to coax another person into a coffin and bury them. It's something entirely different to meet them with violence, to end their existence in such a ferocious manner.

"That's what you want?" I ask him.

"I'm already dying," he says. "The doctors aren't optimistic."

"How long?" I ask.

"Six or seven months, if I'm lucky." He sighs. "I . . . can't kill myself. I can't bring myself to do it. That's why

I came to you. I thought maybe, if you knew what I had done, you'd end things for me."

"You did this so I would kill you?" I ask him. "Because you're too chickenshit to do it yourself?"

Jinx looks away, nodding.

I think for a moment, wondering what to do. Finally, it comes to me—the answer I have been searching for arrives at the front porch of my thoughts and screams at me until hoarse.

I kneel close to Jinx, smearing some of the blood from his hair.

"I'm going to do something horrible to you," I say. "Something you won't ever forget. I'm going to wish you six or seven years. Not months. I'm going to wish you health so that you can endure, so that you can suffer. That's what you truly deserve."

I pick up my rucksack and toss the hammer inside. I think about dressing Jinx's wound and tending to him, but I don't have the desire to. There's something I must do before sunrise, while I am still wrapped in darkness—something I must undo, something I should've never done in the first place.

I make my way toward the schoolhouse door.

"Where are you going?" Jinx asks, straining to lift his head to regard me. "You're leaving?"

"It's almost daylight," I tell him. "We'll be different people then."

He looks at me, mouth hanging open, trying to understand.

"Happy birthday," I say.

Before Jinx can respond, I hurry out of the building and down the steps. I throw my satchel through my van's open window and scramble into the driver's seat. An instant later, I'm twisting the key into the ignition and flying down the dirt road as if my vehicle were powered by jet fuel.

I press on the gas pedal with urgency, the urgency of a fool who's made a careless mistake—a mistake that quite possibly can never be undone.

CHAPTER SIXTEEN

At dark, I become loathsome.

After half an hour or so, I arrive at the remnants of the Hoffman farm on the outskirts of Henley's Edge. I throw the van into Park and topple out of the vehicle, leaving it idling on the edge of the field.

I grab the shovel from the rear of the van and make my way toward the center of the open space. I search for the place where the ground has been disturbed, where I mutilated the earth and delivered another human far too early.

Finally, after searching for several minutes, I come upon the site where the ground has been ripped apart and then hastily caked back together with dirt and uprooted plants.

Without hesitation, I start digging.

The earth seems to pull me farther and farther down as I dig, as dirt flies at the end of my shovel and is flung back into oblivion, back to where even moonlight doesn't dare follow.

"Please," I plead as I dig. "Please be alive."

Finally, the end of the shovel stabs the coffin lid. I'm on my knees in seconds, scrambling to clear the dirt and mud from the lid so that I can open the coffin.

After I've wiped all the dirt from the coffin's lid, I pry it open, silently begging for the old woman to greet me, for her to leap out of her prison and throw her arms around me like a child afraid of the dark.

At dark, I become loathsome.

But when I pull back the coffin lid, none of that happens. The old woman does not stir. She does not spring up from her rest, gasping and clutching for me like a lost toddler. Her eyelids do not flutter open gently as if being roused from an unbearable dream. The old woman does nothing.

She lies there without movement—a sleeping enchantress, far too bewitched by her dreams to part with them and rejoin the realm of the living.

I press my ear against her chest, listening for a heartbeat. But there's no life remaining there now.

Her body is nothing more than an empty vessel—a

sacred pitcher emptied of all contents, what it once contained now smeared across the universe.

This is what I wanted for her. To be free. I wanted to set her free.

But I realized only too late just how misguided my thinking was, how monstrous.

I drag the old woman's lifeless body out of the coffin, out of the grave, until she's lying on the ground beside me. I hold her in my arms and squeeze her tight—wishing I could undo everything I had done, wishing I could somehow bring her back.

I should have never buried her. I should have never done this to her.

I'm a monster.

This much I know.

On the periphery of my vision, I notice two dark silhouettes slowly approaching me. I wonder if it's Pema and Bailey, coming to comfort me, arriving when I need them the most.

I don't look at them.

Instead, I rock the old woman's body back and forth, gently, like a mother cradling a precious newborn.

"Happy birthday," I whisper to her.

The two of us remain there together, my arms wrapped around her corpse, until morning light begins to leach across the field of tall grass, until the sky unravels bright and warm like a wildfire burning up all of heaven.

At dark, I become loathsome.

ACKNOWLEDGMENTS

I'm grateful for many kind souls who made this book's existence possible. First, I owe so much thanks to Marc Gerald and Norman Reedus for their unwavering support and faith in me as an artist. I'd like to thank my brilliant editor, Melissa Ann Singer, for helping me refine so much of this story and for pushing me to create something unique, something truly compelling. I'm also equally grateful for all the very kind and thoughtful people I've worked with at Blackstone—Josie Woodbridge, Ananda Finwall, Sarah Bonamino, Stephanie Stanton, Rachel Sanders, Candice Roditi, etc.

I'm especially grateful for my literary agent, Priya Doraswamy, and my film/TV manager, Ryan Lewis, for guiding me and shaping so much of my future as an author with their care and dedication.

Finally, I owe so much gratitude to my boyfriend, Ali, for always encouraging me when I am low and reminding me to celebrate the many joys of our life together. *I am not as loathsome as I once was because of him . . .*